Paddle Portage Ponder

A travel memoir

By

Perrilee Pizzini

ISBN 9781701161566

ACKNOWLEDGMENTS

I wish to thank the Burien Seniors Writers Workshop participants: everyone has given me guidance, help with editing and encouragement. My writing abilities have improved over the last six years because of their honest and encouraging words. I especially want to thank Sallie Tierney, our leader, for her patience and persistence, and Roberta Jean Bryant for her friendship, advice and counsel.

Perrilee Pizzini

DEDICATION

To my children, grandchildren, great grandchildren
and those that follow, given so they may have a glimpse
into the life of one of their ancestors.

Dana
Mike
Paul
Brandon
Marie
Carl
Kris
Jennifer
Adam
Christopher
Karter
Logan
Landon

Paddle Portage Ponder

A travel memoir

Paddle Portage Ponder

Perrilee Pizzini

August 6, 2017

Million Acres of Wilderness
Overly Excited
Five Great Lakes

Dear Sister Ursula,

Many people are afraid for my safety. They are frightened at the idea of being alone and being without communications. I have quit telling people about my plans because I am tired of explaining the appeal.

My real fear has surfaced. I do not want undesirable men to know where I will be. I do not want to think about the possibility of being followed and stalked by a crazy or aggressive male.

I sit on the porch surrounded by quaking aspen. It is easy to hear why they are named quaking as the round leaves shake in the breeze. They are as I remember from my childhood a happy tree; at least watching their sensual dance makes me happy.

I have expected to be swarmed by Mosquitoes, and I am delighted there are only a few humming nearby. A pair of Goldfinches are eating their fill as they search through seed pod clumps. They come and go enjoying the fluff that is on full display. They do not like it when I swat at the bugs that have discovered my presence.

Here on the edge of civilization, I sit on the porch, wondering what my lessons about life will be. A tiny Chipmunk joins me; he is busy running from place to place. I muse he is a reflection of me getting ready. Always looking for something as he keeps poking his head out, then dashing back into the Sweet Peas that are in full pink and white bloom.

It has turned very dark as I sit. The stars are thick in the sky. So thick, I cannot see any constellations.

I think how and why I am here while I am lying on the basic bunk in a rustic cabin I have rented for the night at my planned boundary entry point. All my provisions are packed and ready to load into the canoe in the morning. I am about to start my two months canoeing through the USA and Canada Boundary Waters. As the thoughts go through my head, it sounds like I am planning on navigating the Great Lakes.

I chuckle and say out-loud to myself. "NO! I am not." The thought scares me more than a little. I could put in at my maternal grandparents' old place in Duluth. It isn't the most western point of the lake, but nearly, just a few miles east, and it would be a memorable location for me. Research would need to be done, but it seems if I were to follow the South Shore, that would be the better choice.

Skip by Lake Michigan flow into Lake Heron on the Soo Canal. Just thinking of taking a canoe, no, that would have to be a kayak trip. Just the idea of being among the thousands of ships is scary, but would it be scary? It is unknown, so more than a bit scary. The lakes are vast, and a kayak would stay within the half-mile of shoreline. The rest of the lake, the center, would be for the ships.

It would be the western shore of Lake Huron, which is probably half the distance than the northern and eastern route. From Lake Huron to Lake Erie, it is the long canals and through Lake Saint Clair and another long channel. I need a map. I think it is a toss-up if the northern or the southern route would be best. My memory is failing me as to the dimensions and locations. I cannot visualize in my mind going from Lake Erie to Lake Ontario. Then it is a long route going through Canada to the Atlantic Ocean on a river. "What river? Think." I cannot believe it takes thinking to remember. In a flash, I remember, "Ahh, yes, it is the Saint Lawrence Seaway." It was dug and made when I was a child.

"Maybe it would be wise to portage the whole trip and go by steamer," I say to myself as I turn out the light to sleep as I think about how dreams start with the thoughts I focus on just before sleep.

I cannot sleep. Even the outrageous fantasy thoughts of paddling the Great Lakes doesn't distract me from the intense anticipation of the trip in front of me. I check out the shelf above the table and find a book. Yup, what else would be on the shelf here but 'The Boundary Waters.' Opening paragraph states—'The boundary waters are in Northeastern Minnesota and Southern Ontario. They are made up of a million acres of wilderness, with hundreds of pristine lakes and streams, and hundreds of miles to canoe and portage through the wilderness.' I am ready. I am giddy with anticipation and excitement. Reading about the area calms me: no ocean-liners, not one large city, no ships and canals or locks to encounter.

I know Sister Ursula you are a stickler for perfection, but I have to capitalize Mosquitoes, Goldfinch, Chipmunk. It is just so disrespectful not to. There will be many more. I will try to be consistent.

Goodnight,
Edna

Birds — Northern Flicker, Golden Finch
Animals — Least Chipmunk
Plants — Quaking Aspen, Sweet Pea
Rustic Cabin at Boundary Water Entry Point
Iron Lake

August 7

Vivid dreams of Dinosaurs drinking water
Same water millions upon millions of years
Alternate sleeping and reading

Dear Sister Ursula,

It is barely light, and I am excited. I walk the short distance to Iron Lake shore where my canoe awaits my departure. I already know the wind is blowing as I have heard it for hours as I lie through the darkness desiring to sleep. I occasionally doze but find I am not able to stay asleep. I dream of kayaking through the Great Lakes. Some dreams are quite scary. I fret while mentally going through everything I have planned; looking for what essential item I have forgotten. I am not as calm as I look at Iron Lake. I contemplate leaving even though the waves are roaring with their white caps straight at me. Frustrated, yes, but more than that, I am feeling the stress of the weeks of preparation, which brings me to the edge of irrational thinking. I go back to the cabin turn on Susan Boyle's CD 'I Dreamed a Dream,' that I had downloaded onto my compute, and choose from the bookshelf Jack London's 'White Fang' and crawl back into bed.

I find I cannot read this depressing, sad tale. I look at the books on the shelf for something else. There is a stack of 'National Geographic Magazines,' a magazine that is too good to throw away. Putting on Yanni's collection, I take the magazines over to the bunk. The cover photo and title 'Water Is Life' catches my eye.

Disappointed, resolved, and remembering that I am warm and dry, I alternate between sleeping and reading. Vivid dreams about the same water we are drinking being drunk by dinosaurs.

It is interesting to think about the fact that there isn't more water or less than was here millions upon millions of years ago here on Earth.

I don't want to unpack, which is foolish as it is planned for the next two months to unpack and repack every day, but I have learned to follow my inner feelings. I walk over to the cafe and order a bowl of Walleye Pike soup. The soup made here at this little cafe is delicious. The Fish in the soup is caught in Iron Lake by the son of the owner. Chunks of fish mixed with small pieces of vegetables in a white sauce. Between bites of soup and delicious bread, that they make at the cafe, I look out at the White Pine tree and watch two Squirrels sitting and eating pine cones. The Squirrels meticulously start at the bottom of the pine cone and take off each scale. Eat the seed one at a time. In short order, there is a pile of scales, and off he goes in search of another. I have no idea what the Crow thought the squirrel had that he would want, but halfway through the second cone, a Crow chases the Squirrel away and checks out the cone. Finding nothing of interest, he leaves it on the ground and flies off. Just harassing the little guy, or did he think that the Squirrel had changed his eating patterns and had something of interest to the Crow?

The soup, actually a chowder, is so good I contemplate getting a bowl for breakfast.

I did nothing today, but I am drained, possibly from lack of sleep. I walk down to check on the canoe, a habit of all boaters--check on the craft even when it is high and dry. Water is still rough. A flock of Canada Geese is hunkered down sleeping. Maybe I will sleep contented tonight.
Goodnight,
Edna
Birds —Common Crow---Animals— Red Squirrel Iron Lake

August 8

Another Beginning
Without ceremony, I load the canoe
I am pleased to be alone

Dear Sister Ursula,

It is still dark when I awake. The sequences of events unfold as expected. I go out and check the weather: the sky is clear, covered with stars, no breeze, Iron Lake is quiet and still. I unplug all of my fully charged electronics. It was an inner debate whether to bring any. For the most part, I will not have any cell or Wi-Fi services. The advantages outweighed the trouble they are to keep dry and protected. With a solar charger and three back up rechargeable batteries, I have all the information I need in one small computer package. I have bird, plant and animal identification, maps, notes on portages, first aid, local history, and thirty books I have always wanted to read or reread and music. I will also use it for inputting information into my diary. I am a woman of the twenty-first century. I came into the electronic era with resistance, but I did arrive. To bring along a plugin keyboard was also a big decision. I knew I would be happy with adding it to the pile. I am also glad I have been using this computer setup for the last month. I am now familiar with it, and it is easy for me to use.

Without ceremony, I load the canoe and paddle on Iron Lake, the first of many. I check the time, five-fifteen. It is only six miles to the first portage. I am pleased that I remembered to drink water. The plan is to drink half a cup of water every half hour--remembering is the problematic part.

I cannot see the portage from a mile out while looking into the cove where the portage is to be, so I choose to paddle along the beach so I will not miss the entrance to the trail. It is not until I am directly in front of the trail that I see it. Because of the gravel and rocks along the shore, hiding the constant use the trailhead gets. Upon arrival at the portage, I check the time, seven forty-five am. No one is at the trailhead — accessible location to take the canoe out of the water. The trail is identified with a six-inch pink ribbon, and from land, I can see that the trail is well used.

I carry my first load of supplies: a large canoe backpack and two food dry bags, one in each hand. Expecting, from my research on the portages, it to be half a mile long and for it to be smooth and flat, but I find it isn't. It is a gentle slope going uphill than a little steeper going downhill with many tripper rocks.

Arriving at Long Lake, I am pleased that no one is here. As I walk back for my next load, I wonder how accurate my notes on the portages are going to be. The distance seems accurate enough, but the trail through not steep or difficult it is not flat and smooth.

The second trip, I carry the canoe on my shoulders on its well-padded yolk. The third trip is another heavy canoe backpack-- the paddles, and three small dry bags. The last trip is the emergency kit and water supply backpack, my lunch/dry bag, and my shoe/boot dry bag.

I check the time, twelve-twenty, reasonable first portage. Only four hours to walk four miles transporting all my gear. While I sit overlooking what is to come, I open the day dry bag and take out my prepared breakfast and morning snack for today: spinach wrap of rice, turkey and cranberries, an oatmeal raisin cookie, a raw carrot, an apple, and a ziplock bag of trail mix.

I eat about half of my breakfast, then load up and check my map. I point the canoe east along the shore for the next portage. Check the time, one-thirty.

As I paddle, I notice the Mallards, I saw them on Iron Lake, but I didn't pay any attention to them as I was so focused on leaving. Now I see that some of these Mallards are not Mallards. I cannot quite recognize what it is about them that is different, but they are not all Mallards. I will check later.

Sun is hot. I feel I am getting too much sun on my exposed skin, though I put on sunscreen before finding the portage I need to get out of the sun to cool down and reapply sunscreen. I am coming up to a small island with trees; I decide to see about making this a rest stop.

It is rocky, but doable to land and not empty the canoe. I step into knee-deep water and pull the canoe up onto a non-sharp rock. By the scuffing of this particular bolder, it is evident that it is often used to secure canoes.

I lay out my lifejacket in the sun to dry the sweaty back. After I wash my face, hair, neck, and arms, I rinse out my sweaty silk blouse and put it back on. While resting, in the shade, I decided to take out my unfinished breakfast and today's lunch. The other half of the turkey sandwich not only looks good I decide I must either eat it or throw it out as it is perishable. My cooling bag works well, but it doesn't have ice, how it cools is by changing the water. Lake water is cold compared to the air. By changing the water several times a day, the food stays fresh. It is only intended to keep food cooler than the air for one day.

I nap and awake feeling refreshed and chilly. Check the time, quarter to five-time to load up, and go the last three miles to the campsite. Paddlers ahead, when I first see them, I think it is two canoes, as they get closer I can tell that it is five canoes. Fortunately, they are coming towards me. I relax as they get close, and I can see that it is families with children.

Friendly group, a child tells me, "We saw a Moose and a Bear."

"When?" I ask.

"Dad was it two or three days ago?" Child asks.

Dad replies, "Moose yesterday morning, the Bear must have been three days ago."

"Maybe I will be lucky enough to see them, too," I reply.

"The portage to Ozada is difficult, take light loads and more trips. Allow plenty of time," warns one of the women.

"Thanks for the information," I say.

The campsite on my map is full. A man comes out to the beach and says. "There isn't much space here, but there is another site around the next point that was empty when we went past it. You will most likely be happier at the other camp spot than sharing this spot with us."

"Thanks, I will look for it. It isn't on any of my information."

"Not on ours either. I think it is an overflow from this one. If for some reason that one doesn't work out, come back and we will squeeze you in."

"Okay, have a great evening," I reply.

The campsite is just around the point and a much better location as it is on the west shore and will get the sun early. I can see why they opted to continue to the other site as this spot is tiny. Perfect for pulling up one canoe. No place for hanging my hammock, but an almost level spot for the tent.

A Kingfisher is working the beach just east of the camp. They are such colorful Birds and such loners. I don't remember ever seeing more than two working an area.

After setting up camp, I assess what chores I need to do. Pumping water to replace what I have drunk today. Hanging the food supply, which I will do after I am done eating for the day, but the first thing is to wash out my sweaty clothes — hanging them on bushes to dry. I take out my leftovers from today's paddling and add them to the snack bag. Dinner is a non-cook meal today. Fresh veggies dipped in seasoned peanut oil. It is only a little after six by the sun, and I wonder what I need to do to celebrate the beginning. I decide to cut into the banana coconut pineapple bread and sing a series of songs starting with 'The Happy Wander, Row Row Row Your Boat, and then How Could Anyone, ending with This Little Light of Mine.' I am surprised that I don't sing more as I paddle.

I open up the Bird ID folder and see that the birds mixed in with the Mallards are American Black Ducks. Though the young, the females of both all look quite the same, the male American Black Ducks are much darker. I learned something today about birds. I never identified an American Black Duck before today; don't remember ever seeing one before today.

Goodnight,
Edna

Birds —Mallard Duck, American Black Duck, Kingfisher
Iron to Long Lake

August 9

Sounds of the Wild
Portage to Ozada is difficult
Distinct footprints in the sand

Dear Sister Ursula,

I awake with a start. I feel fear; noises have unfortunately awakened me. Rustling. Then something is messing with the canoe. I am out of my sleeping bag with my head popped out of the tent in a flash. Four Crows. A relief. I crawl back into the bed. It isn't dark, but it isn't quite light either. I still feel a bit nervous residue of panic in my core. It has been a while since I have been out in the wilderness. I must get used to the sounds of the animals in the wild. Real fear has followed me to this place. I will figure it out, the sounds of what is everyday life here.

Long Lake is smooth as glass. I am up, packed, and on the water at daybreak. My second paddle day, I purposely planned for it to be a short paddle of eight miles. Under two miles to the Ozada portage. Sunrise is uneventful. It was daybreak; then instantly, it is full sun. I notice this because I am disappointed. I am surprised that I have such expectations that I am not noticing the beauty and marvel of the day, but seeing lack.

It only takes a short time to reach the Ozada portage. I accept the advice of the woman who said to take small loads and carry only one large canoe backpack and one small dry sack on the first trip. It is difficult because of the steepness of fifty feet and the potential of tripping on the tree roots. Carefully I observe each step. Instead of the four roundabouts, I end up taking seven because I desire to have one free hand to grab onto the tree branches during the potential problem spots. The fact that it is less than a quarter of a mile long makes it less time-consuming.

I find my watch and it says eleven-thirty, the sun is straight up in the sky, I will not need to check the time when the sun is high in the sky. I am pleased as it is the first time today I have checked the time. I can paddle for many more hours today if I choose. Instead of landing the canoe and getting out to rest and walk, I decide to stretch out and relax in the canoe. I will not sleep, but rest just enough that my legs don't stiffen. I only have another hour and a half to the next portage. The water is so calm I can drift slowly in the direction I desire. I eat an apple and drink water, and while lying back, do my knee stretches. Not a long rest, but long enough that I am ready to paddle more. Though I have memorized this portion of the map, I study the map, and I am sure that the portage site I am looking for is just another mile past the next point.

I pull up to the sandy shore and see vivid human footprints in the sand. I hesitate before getting out. There are no canoes to be seen. They must have moved on. With relief, I land and relax into the process of portaging.

The lake is still, looks like a mirror and the beach has the finest texture. The smoothest possible landing ever. No rocks or logs—powder size grains of sand beautiful. My notes say this portage is only five hundred feet. I divide the gear into piles, similar to the first portage, and start the process of getting all the equipment over to Ozada Lake.

Easy portage, but for some unknown reason I am tired. I decide as I sit with my pile of gear to spend the night here. I am looking forward to resting. This spot is not on any maps, though it is a sanctioned camp spot. Pleasant, and no one is here. The camp spot is small, and by the condition of the ground plants, I can tell it is rarely used because the trail doesn't show signs of being trampled. With the larger recommended camp spot on the maps well marked, I will most likely have this camp spot to my self.

I open a can of chicken; add spices and a packet of Dijon mustard dressing, and make roll-ups with tortilla shells. I spent the evening pumping water, washed out socks and my sweaty shirt and handkerchief, cooking dinner, reading, resting, and listening to music. Start Richard Back's 'Illusions.' I easily become wholly absorbed by the inviting scene of two pilots visiting.

Goodnight,
Edna

Long to Ozada Lake

August 10

Illusions overshadowed
Melodramatic time
Rustling noises awaken

Dear Sister Ursula,

I don't like the feel of sand on my hands, feet, and especially in my sleeping bag. Sister Ursula, you don't seem to mind, but then the sand in your world is underwater, and I don't mind wet sand on the beach. I spend time shacking out and dusting off the sand from everything. As I am cleaning and packing for the day's paddle, a wind comes up, not so much that I couldn't have loaded and gone, but enough that I thought I would wait. Besides, Don and Richard are calling me back to find out how life is an illusion.

The beach is fine sand, but the campsite is moss and other small plants, covering which makes it ideal.

I eat the remaining chicken with added rehydrated peas and carrots.

Wonderful day. The wind died down in the late afternoon, could have paddled on, but decided I would go in the morning. Feeling anxious to get on to the next spot now that I have the Reluctant Messiah's experiences to ponder. Well done, I am pleased with the ending where Richard decides not to follow the avenue of becoming a converter of people by sharing his recent experiences, but to enjoy his life.

Goodnight,
Edna
Ozada

August 11

Tree Frog
This planet is so amazing
Winter Wren

Dear Sister Ursula,

Except for the soft sand, it is a perfect loading. I have an adversity to getting sand in the canoe as well, so I spend time dusting off all the gear and cleaning my water slippers. I do not feel frustrated with the sand but relaxed as it has been a—what? I cannot find just the right word to describe the feeling, fun, comfortable, pretty, ah yes, melodramatic time here on the sandy camp. I feel it has been an exaggerated experience overshadowed by the "Illusion."

Only an hour of paddling, and I am at the campsite for today.

I see large Birds flying over, but I cannot identify them. I am looking into the sun to see them — just black outlines. I keep watching the silhouette—they are Hawks, not big Hawks. I believe they are Red-tails. They are the most common in this area, and it is captivating to watch their graceful acrobatics. Onshore were lots of tweety Birds in the bushes, but couldn't get a good look at any of them. The singing sounds like a Pacific Wren.

It is only a little after noon by the sun, and I wonder what I want to do to celebrate today's short paddle. The map shows a hike to a lookout; I decided to hike the two miles to see what the lookout has to offer. It will be a good workout for my knees. I do a few knee and leg stretches, and I am off.

Entering into the forest, I encounter a vast number of Mosquitoes, I turn back and put on my bug jacket with a hood that covers my face as well, and reenter tracing my steps. The first portion of the trail is a bog, stretching my steps to keep my boots dry even though I have waterproofed them. I do not want to get them muddy. Not realistic as the boots will not leak, but I have a lifetime of keeping dry. I'm not fighting my awkward gate because I want to stay reasonably clean even though it means walking on the edges of the path and rocks that are sticking out of the mud. Sorry Sister Ursula, first the sand now the mud. What an outdoors person I am. I love the woods, but I don't want to be muddy.

It isn't spring, so I am not thinking about Frogs. As I watch my step, I see a little green and brown Tree Frog sitting on the rock I nearly step on it. He is sweet, not knowing of the danger. He just missed being squished by my boot. He is about one and a half inches long. I almost killed him because I don't want to get my boots muddy. It is okay if I am a bit strange. I am so glad I missed killing him.

From the lookout, the day's events for the morning are visible. It looks easy; it is flat and well-traveled. With the bug jacket on, I can enjoy the time sitting among the bushes looking around vigilantly afraid of missing something. Found a patch of Wild Blueberries, had to lift the bug face screen to eat the delicious treat. Glad a Bear hasn't found this patch.

Looked up Pacific Wren - my computer says there are Winter Wrens here by the description. They are very similar in looks and songs to the Pacific Wren. So I will believe The Cornell Bird ID and claim Winter Wren by sound. Another new bird identified.

Goodnight,
Edna

Birds - Red-Tailed Hawk, Winter Wren by song.
Animals—Tree Frog
Mosquitoes
Plants – Blueberries

Ozada to Meadow Lake

August 12

Happy Birthday to Me
Abundance of life
Rainbow Trout a tasty treat

Dear Sister Ursula,

Last night in my hammock while thinking about turning 69. I decided to celebrate my day by staying another day at Meadows Lake. To not paddle—not do anything but look at the abundance of my life.

I futzed around camp went for a little walk, spent hours staring out at the lake. I went out on the lake and fished when I saw a few Fish picking Bugs off of the surface — managed to get one Rainbow Trout into the boat and cooked over an open fire — a tasty treat. Lots of Birds, a few Bugs—put on the bug suit for the hike in the woods. A short walk, the trail didn't go far along the beach.

I love it here so beautiful; this planet is so amazing. I do worry about what we humans are doing to it. In only a couple of hundred years, we have made the earth (that was perfect for humans to live: air, water, plants, animals, everything we need to be healthy) into a catastrophic reality. We as humans may not make it another hundred years. Now we have all but destroyed our air, water, and food supply. The earth will survive, but it looks like it may be the end of humans on earth. Like other species, we will become extinct. People have been on earth for six million years. Humans like us have been around for about two hundred thousand years. Now in two hundred years, we have done so much damage to the earth; it is a possibility we will

19

not survive. If any humans survive I fear it will be the greedy and self-centered, ruthless people who will begin the next civilization. Enough of this thinking—how did it get here? I am taking the canoe out on a look around to get back into feeling good.

Great ride, watched Loons, caught a Walleye Pike, saw a Hawk, not sure what kind. Feel like I opened my eyes again to the beauty of this planet. It doesn't seem possible that the earth is in trouble here, where everything is so pristine and almost untouched.

Goodnight,
Edna

Plants — aware of the abundance of beauty

Meadow Lake

August 13

Socializing Lesson
Beautiful Earth
Canoe on Shoulders

Dear Sister Ursula,

After an hour of paddling, I spot three canoes heading for the portage. They have unloaded their canoes and are taking their first load when I land. Partway through the trees on the trail with my canoe on my shoulders, they come back for another gathering of provisions.

"Hi, where are you headed?"

"To the end of this portage," I say.

"No, I mean, tell us about your travel plans."

I cannot believe them. I have my canoe on my shoulders, and they want to stop and chat. They are blocking the trail. I say, "After I have my canoe delivered and come back for my gear, I will be happy to chat."

"Oh, sorry," says the guy with arms the size of my leg. "I didn't think. We'll catch up with you later."

I am in pretty good shape and have practiced carrying my canoe around, but I don't ever think just holding the canoe and chatting is fun. Possibly my attitude of meeting up with people is an attitude problem I need to adjust. Maybe the portages are a place to gather and exchange information, and a place to have a social experience. Practicing standing and chatting should become part of my flexibility training, and remember that I am not the only person out here enjoying the woods.

When I get to the end of the portage trail, there are three women making lunch — the other half of the three canoes. I physically relax, knowing that the men have their wives with them. I realize just how paranoid I am; I wave at them. I go back for my second load and meet up with the guys who are packing and sorting gear into piles — reminding me of how easy it is to travel alone. The big guy comes over to where I am gathering my gear and says. "Sorry, I should have offered to carry your canoe instead of thinking you are an ox, like me. Would you like help to transport your gear?"

"No, I am fine moving my gear on this easy portage. If it were up and over a cliff as it spells out in the guide book I will be doing in a few days, I would accept your help."

"I don't know if we are going that way or not. I didn't plan the route. I just figured if Danny over there, pointing with his chin at his friend, figures he can do it, I certainly can." He says this loud enough that it is obvious he wants his friend to hear.

I had not planned to stop and rest at this time of day. The portaging is enough time from paddling, but the six are friendly and wanting to share their experience and learn about mine. I stay and snack as they cook their main meal of the day. I am intrigued by this group. Danny is a small guy, almost as little as me, which makes his friends give him a teasing. He is an accountant who doesn't do much exercising. His wife, Darleen, is in great physical shape, tall and robust. She is the one who carried their canoe. No one said what the illness is that Danny has, but it is apparent that they are all delighted that he is well enough to make the trip. Fun to witness three tight couples who are long-time friends.

Danny's wife points out a Cedar Waxwing up in the Spruce tree and says, "What could a seed eater find to eat in that pathetic tree?"

It is time I load up and paddle off on Bug Lake. Having adjusted my attitude towards other people existing out here in the wilderness made the encounter fun. That and it was three couples and not just men.

An easy day of paddling found campsite without effort. I listened to an Owl throughout the evening. Hoo Hoo Hohooooo. 'Who cooks for you?' Barred Owl. I have heard this owl before; maybe I will see it tomorrow and look up who says, 'Who cooks for you?' So I can verify the identification. I don't always verify, sometimes I trust my memory.

I considered how to set up camp so that I can see the lake, canoe, and food stash from my hammock, so the noises from the night can be addressed to ease my mind without getting out of bed.

I don't need a campfire to cook, so I sit in the dark and watch the water lapping the shore. I hear a single crashing in the woods. There is no wind, I think it is a tree limb falling, but it has me feeling uncomfortable. I turn off the old-time classics, so I can listen and know if there are any more sounds. Silence is what I hear.

Goodnight,
Edna

Bird — Barred Owl (by sound) Cedar Waxwing
Plant - Spruce
Meadow to Bug Lake

August 14

The Loon
Red Squirrel sniffing water jug
Mosquitoes - Hidden Figures - Vivaldi

Dear Sister Ursula,

Noises in the night — still a problem. I had to get out of
the hammock to see a Red Squirrel sniffing the water jug. I will
do better tonight.

I woke thinking about having some of the banana bread. So
I shall have the remaining banana bread and trail mix with
peanut butter.

As I eat my breakfast, a group of gulls passes over. It is
difficult to know if they are Herring Gulls or California Gulls as
they look so much alike, and I cannot see if they have yellow or
pink legs. I believe them to be Herring Gulls as they are the
most abundant here.

Here on Bug Lake, there are fewer bugs than there were at
Meadow Lake on my hike, but enough to don my bug suit.

A male Loon popped up five feet from the canoe. I
followed it around for a long time. It was staying up quite a
while, then ducking down, then staying down an even longer
time. After following the Loon around for a few dives, I started
timing this loon. His pattern was to be up - three to five minutes,
then dive and stay down about five to six minutes. The Loon
kept ducking down and coming up fifty feet from the spot it
went down, in a wobbly circle. Not coming back up in the area it
was before. My study is a small one, only eighteen dives. Musing
about saying a Loon is ducking. People duck underthings to
keep from hitting their head, but somehow to say a Loon is

ducking sounds incorrect — ducks duck. Playing with the Loon is an omen. The beginning of playing on this outing, something I need to allow myself.

I think Loons are ventriloquists. At least it is difficult to spot the direction from where the sound is coming. I did hear Loons calling, but not the one I was following; he didn't make a sound while I was with him. I am not sure of that; they seem to make their musical haunting tune without effort. He seemed unbelievably uninterested in me, didn't always go further away from me. I kept trying to guess where he was going. Amazingly unsuccessful at anticipating his direction. He came up very close to me one more time. I just sat still with my paddle resting on my lap.

The portage today was very easy. A few bugs, but not bad. Short about a hundred and fifty feet, flat, Bug Lake beach was sandy, Ojibway has small gravel. No people.

A five-mile paddle on Ojibway Lake and camped in a busy, buggy campsite. So many bugs I put up the tent on a thick, soft Moss as it is easier for me to kill Mosquitoes in the tent than the hammock. I cannot find this Moss on the computer—If I was the Moss, how would I define myself? I am the color of sage, I have tiny white flowers with four petals-- and I do not have a stiff stem.

I am listening to Vivaldi as I write to you, Ursula. I am not getting out of the tent now until morning. I hung my food, leaving out just enough for what I will eat tonight. I will eat it all. I brushed my teeth earlier as I will stay in the tent.

I turned off the music, and I am about to start 'Hidden Figures' by Shetterly.

Skipped the daily chores today, didn't do laundry, cook, charge batteries, or pump water. I did tie the food up in a tree near the water.

Perrilee Pizzini

A Regal Creature

He is a Loon— Majestic, yes — But just a Bird
My heart quickens — With the sitting
Of his speckled presence
I sit in my canoe — Watching — Waiting
The Loon appears — I hold my breath
In reaction to his beauty
He gracefully floats — I float — He vanishes
I paddle — Guessing — Where will he show
There — excited — Gently paddling — Towards him
He pays no attention — Resting — Immersion
Guessing again — Where? — Propelling
He surfaces — Gracefully — Riding the waves
Mesmerized — I sit back relaxed — Listening to his call
He looks at me — Indifferent — He dives
I continue to follow — He continues — His Pattern
Disappearing-- Into the Underwater world
Surfacing at will
A random pattern — I assume to — Discourage detection
I am not satisfied — With only glimpses — Into his world
I desire a connection — To this regal creature
Knowing he is just a Bird

Goodnight,
Edna

Birds — Common Loon, Herring Gull
Plants - Beautiful Soft Sage colored moss
Bug to Ojibway Lake

August 15

Black Bears mama with four cubs
Rolling over borders
Bald Eagles
I am surprised - no Raccoons

Dear Sister Ursula,

A whole day without even a glimpse of a canoe or person.
I did see Black Bears — a mama with her four cubs. The cubs are small, but then Mama Bear is probably only three hundred pounds. They were on the beach among boulders. I stopped paddling the moment I saw a brief movement of black fur. They were all behind rocks from my viewpoint. Paddling about fifty feet offshore, I stopped to watch the Bears weave in and out from behind the boulders. All black and about the same size: rocks and the little Bears looked very similar, except the Bears never stopped moving. It looked like they were playing with the stones, but then it also looked like they were eating something they found under the rocks.

It was a combination of playing and eating. Considering the size of the Bears and the size of the berries, grubs, and bugs they eat, it is only logical that they eat while at play, or is it play while they eat?

The four cubs were in constant motion. For a long time, I thought there were only two cubs until they were all in view at the same time. It must be challenging for her to keep an eye on so many and to feed them. Mama didn't look like she was playing. She was rolling over large boulders and eating. Don't know for sure what, but my guess she is eating bugs.

When I went to shore later, several miles from where I saw the Bears, I rolled over boulders to see what was under them. Bugs, many bugs. Many different kinds. I don't study insects or identify them. I am just not that interested. I categorize them as spiders, beetles, centipedes, worms, ants, rolly-pollies, mites, and winged though I do know some of the flying ones. Mosquito, White Socks, No-see-um, Horse Fly, and Termite.

The portage to Elbow Lake was long, almost a mile one way, but easy walking. Tied the paddles inside the canoe and the small dry bag with the empty water bottles and wore the small backpack while carrying the canoe. I am pleased that I made it on three trips instead of four. I will do it again. Knowing I had this long portage, I didn't pump water last night or this morning, which helped with the small backpack weight. I had plenty for all day. Still had a liter after the portage.

Sister Ursula, while I was pumping water, I saw Bald Eagles. A pair is coming and going to a nest up on the top of a dead Pine Tree. A bit disappointed that I didn't see the Eaglets. It is in my nature to want more.

Elbow Lake is named well, it is a perfect forty-five-degree elbow, coming in one end paddling to the other end for the next portage. The campspot is right at the bend. Not many bugs tonight, I will set up the hammock.

I recognize the little Squirrel noises and the Crows and little tweety Birds. So, now there are some disturbances I recognize, which enables me to ignore them; which means I do not get up to see what is happening. But I still need to check on the wind, waves, and odd louder noises I hear. I have worked on the rigging of the cord to the flap at the foot of the hammock. When I pull on the rope tied to the tarp near my left hand, it picks up the tarp so I can see the canoe and food cache directly in front of me. The lake is seen a little bit through the trees, but I cannot see the waves.

I am surprised that there aren't Raccoons, so I looked it up in my little computer library. What I found is that there isn't a reliable food source through the winter, and Raccoons do not do as well in conifer forests.

I am looking forward to reading a bit more about these amazing black women mathematicians.

Goodnight,
Edna

Birds - Bald Eagle pair
Animals - Black Bears (Mama and four cubs), Bugs
Plants - Balsam Fir

Ojibway to Elbow Lake

August 16
Whitetail Deer Antlers bobbing in and out
A whole day without people

Dear Sister Ursula,

It is another beautiful day, clear blue skies. I started the day
by pumping water, cooking cornmeal, and washing out clothes.
I'm all packed up for the long paddle to the portage to Phantom.
All good intentions followed the shore for about three miles and
decided to get out and do a little exploring on the very green
field I had seen for the last half hour.

Desirable beach with small rocks and a scattering of round
boulders. Couldn't see any footprints on the shore in the gravel
and midsize rocks. I walked up to the field, looked like a trail
leading through the middle of the open area. To my great delight
and surprise, I found large Deer prints. Keeping to the well-used
path, I encountered many piles of large droppings. Small for Elk,
but substantial. I am contemplating whether they are small Elk
or what when I hear crashing through the woods off towards the
lake.

I stand still and wait for the Deer to come out of the woods,
but nothing happens, the crashing stops, and I see nothing. I
continue to walk away from the lake through the field. About six
hundred feet in front of me is a bare spot, possibly a rock.
Breaking off of the trail, I come to a fast rock, nothing growing
on it. The highest place on the stone is about three feet higher
than the grass covered ground, this gives me a little viewing
point above the tall grass. No breeze to keep the Bugs away, I
slip on my bug jacket and pull up the hood. I sit and sip on my
tea and have a bit of trail mix. Through my binoculars, I check
on the canoe. It is reassuring to see it as I left it, no sign of
anything but Birds flying in the bushes, two small Hawks,

overhead circling with the Gulls and off in the distance big
Birds, maybe Eagles or maybe Great Blue Herons. I had a
couple of flashes that looked like feet trailing behind, but they
are too far away to identify.

I scan the field just above the grass; my heart beats a little
faster as I spot brown fur though the binoculars, maybe an Elk
or Deer. I don't see it without aid. I pack up and walk towards
the location of the animal, angling towards another bald spot I
believe to be another rock all the time watching for movement. I
haven't hunted for many years. Sitting on a trail with plenty of
Deer sign was my method. Read a book and wait for the Deer to
come to me. I am not trying to get a shot. I want to see them,
running away would be just fine, but I would prefer to see them
grazing.

I arrive at the spot I thought would be a rock, and it is. Lots
of droppings, I have lived in western Washington for half a
century, and I am used to the little coastal Deer who's little
round droppings are half the size of a dime. What I find is
monstrous in comparison. Again I scan the field just above the
grass, I see the canoe, and it is only awaiting my return. Then in
my binocular view is a set of antlers. In my excitement, I cannot
hold the binoculars still, so I cannot count the points. Deep
breaths and I calm down; he isn't moving, he is just chewing. I
have time to relax. He is closer than I had expected, but he is
still a comfortable distance away. The grass is tall; I cannot see
his legs and the lower half of his body. He is big, definitely a
Deer and not an Elk. I count eight points. I don't see any gray
on his face; he looks young, his fur has a reddish tint to it.
Beautiful animal, he seems unconcerned with me watching him.
He must know it is several months before hunting season.

I pull out my tea and eat a pancake sandwich that has
peanut butter and raisins. Unlike the Bear, he doesn't sniff the

air or be endlessly moving about; this guy eats and walks a few feet and eats. Appears to be lackadaisically unconcerned. He stared towards me as he ate, but has changed direction and has moved away from me one step at a time. I watch his butt, but the grass has been tall, and I haven't seen the white flash that will tell me it is a Whitetail Deer, I am not sure if there are Mule Deer here or whitetail. I need a quick look at his butt to verify, I remember the difference in their antlers. This one does not have the peace sign with its points. Meaning it is a Whitetail. The Whitetail Deer has a black tail, and the Mule Deer has a white tail and rump like an Elk, only not quite so big.

I am out of drinking water, and I am wanting to head back to the canoe and get paddling. As I load up my gear, I drop my water bottle, and it makes a metallic clunk sound startling the Deer, and he bounds off with his nonwhite rump showing. Well, there it is— settled, a Whitetail Deer.

I spent all day watching the open field and the Deer antlers bobbing in and out of the grass — a very well-spent day.

I managed to paddle for two hours; making it to the campsite before dark and before a group of ten pulled in shortly after I arrived. So, at least in my opinion, the only one that matters, I had the best spot, and they crammed in everywhere. Noisy, funny, and exuberant. Music was blaring, kids busy building a fire, parents making dinner and getting the tents and tarps up. It is so easy to travel alone.

I have retreated to my hammock to read about NASA treating the black women poorly. But that isn't any surprise.

Goodnight,
Edna
Animal – Whitetail Deer   Elbow Lake

August 17

Hoisting up cliff
Turkey Vultures scan the sky
Ugly bird

Dear Sister Ursula,

The family has been here with their mama. Left some
footprints on the trail that was probably made by the Bears along
the lake. It doesn't go very far before it becomes only three feet
high through the brambles. Honestly could be another family,
but there are so many baby prints and only occasionally an adult
print. It is a short distance from where I saw the four cubs and
their mama yesterday--it is most likely them.

Another beautiful hot day. I am only going to do one
portage today at the end of the day. There is a camp spot at the
portage point on Phantom Lake and another about five miles
past the portage. Best to decide after the move to Phantom. The
notes on this move say it has two possibilities over the hill and
through the swamp. It depends on the water level, which is the
best choice. Paddling through the swamp is not an option. Some
years it is dry other years difficult. Good notes on this portage.

It is still a day paddle to the trailhead to Phantom, with only
one more campsites on this side of the lake. It is an amazingly
round lake, I will take the western shore.

I am looking forward to the day. I will write later and see
how it went.

While packing lunch and dinner in the daypack for easy
access--mostly jerky and trail mix for the day, and I put to soak
dehydrated chicken stew in a thermos for dinner. It only needed
to heat it for a few minutes and it was ready. I had fun making

the food for the trip. The most challenging part was figuring out how much to pack for each meal — not wanting to have leftovers if possible and yet having enough food for each meal. Paddling takes energy. I paddle about three miles an hour, figuring three to seven hours a day. A lot of energy used. So far, I am pleased with the portions I prepared.

Well, what can I say about today? On the eastern side of the lake, there were lots of birds, big ones. I think Buzzards, must have been something big dead or dying. Too far across to see clearly. On my side, I kept looking for Bears, didn't see any today. I stopped for lunch at an almost sandy beach--more like pea gravel. Walked up a trail through the woods, though it might break out to a vista twice when the trees opened up to the sky, but it stayed in the woods. Not sure where the trail was headed--turned around at a swampy, muddy area. Heard a few Frogs, but didn't see any. I didn't have any idea if I was near the top of the hill or not.

People were camped at two of the designated campsites. Paddled the whole twenty-two miles to the portage; I passed an oncoming group of four canoes a couple of miles before getting to the trailhead. I was close, following the shore; they were out in the middle, too far away to converse. No one was at the portage, pulled in and unloaded the canoe. With the gear in a pile, I walked around to explore the swamp and hillside possibilities. It is quite apparent that everyone was going over the hillside. I walked to the swamp, which looked like the overgrown edges of lakes that are impossible to paddle. The hill was not steep for the first quarter-mile; then, it became quite steep for 300 feet. Evident that people were piling their gear along the trail where it gets tricky. Probably groups are making brigades, passing bundles from one to another over the hill. Not comfortable walking. Rough, need to watch each step. The hill going down is long and a gentle easy trail. Near the bottom of the hill, it meets up with the swamp trail that is wide and well worn.

Three trees have been used as pulleys by others to pull the gear up the short cliff. I have a rope, and I rigged it up and was successful at hoisting the lighter loads. My problem was being alone; I needed to do both the top and the bottom. Each trip down to tie more baggage; I carried several of the heavier bags up the trail. The canoe was too heavy for me to pull up the cliff, so I put it on my shoulders as usual. As I look at the grooves in the dirt at the top of the cliff, it is evident that some people have pulled the canoes up the cliff, but I am not even going to try.

I am not sure it was more accessible, but fun to see if I am strong enough to pull up some of the lighter bundles. My arms are tired from pulling them up the hill. Also, my legs are tired from packing the loads up such a steep incline. I managed to get all of it to the top before people started to come up the trail from Phantom.

My stuff was scattered along the trail—I apologized and gathered everything into a pile out of the way. They were friendly enough, saying the usual stuff; hello, lovely day, hot out today. Young men, maybe, in their late twenties. Lots of them, maybe ten. They didn't even stop to assess the hill, just kept going, amazing to watch the athletic young do so effortlessly what I work so hard at to accomplish. I took six loads to get everything down from the top of the hill and to Phantom Lake. They were all gone by the time I finished.

I had another lunch and took a short nap, about an hour before I loaded up and paddled to the first camp spot. To my relief, it was empty, and this is the most tired I have been. The portage was tough. Today was about pulling things up, and I am not in the condition to do that.

Perrilee Pizzini

I looked up Buzzards and found that here in the USA, the common Turkey Vulture is known as the Buzzard. Ugly bird—it has no feathers on its head and neck to help keep it healthy. They only eat dead animals that have begun to rot, and all the dead things it consumes are bacteria-ridden, so, by having a naked neck, it is easier to keep the diseases from transporting on to their skin. To tell it from other Vultures, the Turkey Vulture (Buzzard) has a very redhead.

No music, no reading. Just sleep.

Goodnight,
Edna

Birds - Buzzard (Turkey Vultures)
Elbow to Phantom Lake

August 18

Laughs at my pain and misery
Glad to be of assistance
Cold Feet

Dear Sister Ursula,

I was thinking early today; I should have brought you along with me. All this freshwater, you would love it as I do. People would think I had lost my mind.

I can see the headlines —"Crazy Old Woman Takes Her Old Pet Gold Fish With Her On A Canoe Trip." If for no other reason I should have because it is so funny. Maybe I am losing it--what an idea-- the thought of bringing you along. I don't know if you would have enjoyed today's paddle. Here is how it went.

Four Crows fly in and land on the rock where I am making my breakfast. I yell, "NO! You don't get any. That is my food." They fly to the treetop and talk. Three of them come down noisily attacking my gear. As I am shooing them away and gathering my positions into a pile under the canoe, the fourth quietly steals my bag of flax seed crackers. I have always know Crows are smarter than me. Proved to me as they absconded with three meals worth of rye crackers.

My first personal wild animal encounter, and I am having to learn from them to not have my gear scattered around. It is vital to keep it safe as I need all of it.

There was a bit of a breeze as I launched. With the rocky shore, I started the day with wet feet. I had rolled my pants up to above my knees, so they stayed dry. But my feet are cold. For

37

two hours all I thought about was finding a place to land to dry
my feet and put on dry socks. I was not thinking well. There
weren't any good landing and launching locations — no place
where I could launch and keep my feet dry. With my single
focus, I missed thinking about solving the problem. How it came
to me, I don't know, but in an instant, it dawned on me to land
anywhere and get my dry socks.

I did just that, landed, dug out my dry socks, two plastic
bags, and my elastic sleeve garters. I reloaded into the canoe with
my wet feet. I took off my wet water booties, wet socks, and
dried my feet with my handkerchief. Put on my dry wool socks,
put plastic bags on my feet secured with the sleeve garters and
picked up my paddle, and admired the beautiful day.

I will not get caught in this situation again. Lesson two, and
it is only nine am. I have had cold wet feet before, In fact, most
of the time canoeing and kayaking it is planned to have wet feet,
but for some reason, it just was unacceptable today. Before I
landed for lunch, I put my dry socks and garters in my day dry
bag. I put on my wet socks and water shoes and walked through
the knee-deep water to shore.

I reach the Toe Lake portage later than I had planned. Toe
is not shaped like a toe, so I have no idea where this lake earned
its name. It is another short portage, only a quarter of a mile. My
notes say it is full of tripping stones. I can see it is full of people
going both directions. From where did they all come? There is
not enough room to handle this many canoes. As soon as I see
what is happening, I decide to paddle away and explore the
swampy area at the very end of the lake. Good Moose swamp. I
don't see any Moose.

I do find six pairs of Red-Winged Blackbirds. I hear them
first, then paddle right up to the shallow weeds growing in the
lake and on purposeful display are the males with red shoulder

patches flying away from their nests trying to lure me away. The contrast of the red and yellow on the back is stunning.

Several canoes are leaving the portage area, so I paddle back up to the portage. Only one canoe is on the beach and no people. I pull in and unload my canoe and do the preparation work for the portage. A guy shows up to carry a canoe and says, "Hello, it has been a zoo here with all the canoes. The portage trail is narrow and wet. Cannot pass with canoes, difficult with large packs. Two canoes are coming this way, you can take a load of gear, but best to wait on taking the canoe until they get done. I am going to wait until they get here before I take my canoe."

"Hi," I say, "Thanks for all the information. This is the first portage I have been with so many people. How far is the muddy part of the portage, and how deep is the water?" I ask.

"Not deep, from three to six inches and some muddy areas. Almost all the way is muddy and wet."

"The information I have says it is a thousand feet, less than a quarter of a mile; also says it is muddy when it rains. It must be higher water now than usual. I see you have mud to your knees."

"Yup, I slipped and managed to fall, carrying one of the canoes. Fortunately, I didn't get hurt, nor did I damage the canoe. Soft mud and water where I landed on my knees. Just lucky. We are taking more trips to keep our gear clean. Our first loads are a mess. Sometimes we slipped, and sometimes we fell; we had to put things down into the mud and come back and retrieve them. We had totes scattered all over the trail, as each of us had taken more than we could carry."

I started laughing so hard I couldn't continue working preparing for the portage.

He says, "Why are you laughing? It was mud everywhere. My youngest was stuck, couldn't move; he had to drop all of his load into the sloppy mud. The older two teens volunteered to go back and gather all the dirty things, and they did an excellent job. If it was just a little deeper, we could drag the canoes empty over the trail. At least that is the joke we are telling."

"You are a wealth of information. How many are there in your group?"

"Nine of us, two children. Of which one is a passenger, my six-year-old son. He has been a real trooper. We are two families, which are the four adults, three strong, capable teenagers, and the two children. I made a deal with my wife after our first trip to the other end of this trail. If she managed to get the children clean and fed, the dirty gear somewhat de-muddy I would carry the rest of our gear over."

"Who got the better end of that deal?" I asked.

"We will be discussing that for the rest of our lives." He laughs, "I don't know. I do know that feeding the kids is the easiest part as I made lunches last night, so every one of us has a bag with our names on it. Passing them out and organizing drinks is all there is to do. Drinks are a big challenge. The kids don't drink straight water, and getting the kids to hydrate is a challenge we didn't think about ahead of time. She is better at getting the kids to help than I am. They were all cleaned up, with clean, dry clothing on and eating when I left on the last load. I love this water, no chlorine added. Tastes so good. We have three pumps, and it is a pleasure to pump the water for the group."

I am having a difficult time talking as I am laughing so hard. He is non-stop entertaining. I get out between chuckles, "She is probably over there taking a nap while you continue."

"I have done eighteen trips, counting this last canoe. Herb, the other dad, has done eleven. His teen boys can do more than my two younger. My teen son made six trips. As I said, we learned to take small loads. Most of our gear did not get very muddy. Only the first load was dripping with mud."

"You are a good story, teller. You have kept me laughing for the half-hour while preparing for the hike and waiting for the incoming."

"Here comes the first canoe." He gets up and helps the man lower the canoe off of his shoulders.

While listening to the portage story, I have unloaded my canoe and moved it up out of the way for the canoes that will be launching. The second canoe arrives. I load up my canoe backpack and head down the trail to Toe Lake. It is a sloppy mess. The ground under the muck is solid. I have very little trouble walking to the other end. I empty my canoe backpack onto some dry and clean grass and take the empty portage-pack back with me to Elbow Lake. Load up one food dry sack and a couple of the small packs into the pack and trod back through the muck to Toe. Then I do it again and again. On my way back empty, I meet my canoe halfway.

"What are you doing carrying my canoe?" I ask the talkative guy.

"I didn't know what to do with myself; if I stayed, I would have to load the canoes. Figured it would be easier to carry another canoe," was the reply.

"Thank you, but..."

"I know you could have done it," he said. "We have held you up at least two hours. I saw you leave when you saw all of us here and entertain yourself at the swamp. The least I could do. When you get back come and meet my wife and kids."

With my last load in the pile and my feet, pants and arms washed, I walked over to meet the group. "Hi," I say to the group.

The guy says, "This is the woman who laughs at my pain and misery."

"Hi, I'm Jane. My husband loves anyone who will laugh at his stories. You have made him a delighted man. He didn't have a good day until he was able to entertain you. When you showed up and began laughing at him as he told of the difficulties this portage provided, it changed his perspective on the day. Thank you. He hadn't seen it as funny until you started to laugh at the situation he was describing."

"I am glad I could be of assistance. With all the schlepping he did, well, all of us have done today, it is good to see the humor in it. I will admit I wasn't looking forward to carrying the canoe through the muck."

While they loaded and launched, I repacked and organized my gear. I was tired and decided to take a short rest, allowing the group to move ahead. As I relaxed and enjoyed the silence of the afternoon, I enjoyed the sound of nuthatches tweeting in the bushes. Looking over towards the bushes, I could see glimpses of them moving about.

Slept a long time; hungry when I awoke, and the sun in the sky indicates it is later than dinner-time. I think about how easy it is to travel alone and how much work is it to travel of any kind with children. Decisions so easy alone.

Stayed instead of going on to the next portage.

Goodnight,
Edna

Birds - Nuthatch, Red-Winged Black Birds,
Plants - Vine Maple
Phantom to Toe Lake

August 19

Red-Winged Black Birds Stunning
Roasted Chestnuts sound special
Osprey

Dear Sister Ursula,

Toe Lake has swampy edges, and the Red-Winged
Blackbirds line the sides. The males sing from the top of the
swamp reeds; a unique and lovely sound continues to the Moose
portage. The group is camped at the campground about a half
mile before the trailhead to Moose, I pull in close to shore, "Hi,
staying here another day.?"

"Yup," said Jane. "We found we are all in agreement. We
are tired and want to stay here another day. I decided to pop
some popcorn and roast a few chestnuts for lunch. You are
welcome to join us."

"Thanks for the invite. I am going to hit the trail to Moose
Lake, planning to put in a little more effort looking for Moose
following the shore. I heard that the lake has a lot of Moose and
I'll spend the night on Moose Lake. Maybe I will even see a
Moose."

"Good luck."

"Roasted chestnuts sounds special."

"It is a long portage between Toe and Moose. Have fun,"
echoes across the water.

The camping area is full of people, so I don't go near, just
keep paddling. Found a well used small camp spot around a
couple of points that must be there by necessity and used as an

overflow. It has a western view, which should be good for the sunset.

I forgot to write about the Osprey circling off in the distance yesterday. The Osprey's silhouette is very distinctive. Today I saw the pair again. I think these are the same Birds; it is the same area, but I am miles closer. They are hunting for food. So graceful, quick movements for a large Bird.

Goodnight,
Edna

Birds - Osprey - Red-Winged Black Birds

Toe to Moose Lake

August 20

Plantain Weed Seeds
Searching for Moose
Fairyland

Dear Sister Ursula,

Spent the day paddling around Moose Lake. The whole thing, I left the camp set up and took the day looking for Moose. I didn't see any trace of a Moose. A well spent the day.

Stopped for a stretch and a hike up a short trail - successful walk saw Bear tracks on the beach, both small and large. They must have spent a little time here as there were several piles of scat, and the rocks on the edge of the water had been turned over. Unlike the old country westerns movies, I have no idea how old the prints are, I am not a tracker — no sighting of an actual Bear.

Only a few Bugs, not bad. Eating the seeds of the Plantain is doing its trick, only a couple bites today.

I cannot believe how many Red Winged Blackbirds I saw today — not lined up like in the early spring with the females sitting on nests, but everywhere in the marshes. I am looking forward to seeing a Moose. I cannot understand my obsession with wanting to see a Moose. I've not even seen a print all day, but then tracks are not seen in the water nor from the canoe.

Lunch and break food were uninteresting; I was lazy this morning and didn't pack lunch just brought trail mix and more trail mix; didn't even pack any jerky. Afternoon stretch, I dug through my daypack and found some nuts and two pieces of jerky. Better. Walking around, I found a sweet little creek. Decided to pump water here at this spot because it is like a bit of fairyland, perfectly set stones with moss growing on and around them with little flowers an inch in height, and the flowers are an eighth of an inch in diameter. It is like a water station designed to entice drinking. But I don't just drink the water, or even taste it. I pump the water. Was it only by coincidence that I thought to throw in the water backpack with all the empties, or was it an omen or premonition? Maybe it was because I brought the empties that I take advantage of this lovely spot to pump water. I think that the thoughts going through my head has been influenced by having read about the reluctant messiah. I so rarely have taken the canoe out without all my belongings on this trip I cannot say if it is a usual decision. Today's synchronicity has been as if not planned a desirable diversion from my looking for a Moose.

I had put to soak before leaving this morning on my Moose hunt—a small amount of dried strawberries, blueberries, bananas, and pears. I have been thinking about them for the last five hours. I hope they taste as good as my mind thinks they will.

As I sit here eating my fruit salad listening to the tweety Birds sing, I am so grateful for this time on the water and being with the woods.

Goodnight, Sister Ursula.
Edna

Plants- Plantain Weed Seeds to repel Mosquitoes
Moose Lake or as I have begun to think of it as Not A Moose In Sight Lake.

August 21

Successful against odds
Hidden Figures
They just ignored me

Dear Sister Ursula,

Read about black women beating the odds and working for
NASA. Unbelievable to me that these intelligent women found a
way to be so academically successful against odds that are so
large, it is difficult to imagine, that each figured out how to make
a career with NASA — inspiring.

A group of three couples came and set up came in the early
afternoon. Decided to pack up and move to the next camp, the
map says there is one about four miles towards Larch Lake.

There is no breeze; the water is like a mirror. The sun is
glistening on the water, and I am paddling. Perfect Day.

But the best thing is that because I left I had a gift on the
way. I spot a Bird on a stob. There was a forest fire here about
ten years ago, so there are many dead trees and partial trees
everywhere sticking out above the young foliage. I head down
the bay to check out the Bird, as I draw closer I can see it is
large, probably an Owl or a Hawk. I don't have my binoculars
within arms reach, no reason why; I continue to glide closer.
There is no movement; I decide that what I see is wishful
thinking. Then I think it is a Bird, as I move a bit to my right, I
think it is a Bird. Then, it is not a Bird but an illusion. I am as
close as I can get. Okay, it is time for a final decision. It is the
top of the dead tree trunk. With my active imagination, I have
created a Bird. I turn the canoe away from shore to continue my
journey to the portage.

I hear an air sound out of the stillness. Yes, an Owl. Easily identified as it flies directly in front of me with the sun behind me. A perfect view of its' brown-and-white-striped feathers, no ear tuffs, about the size of a Crow, but much rounder. Except for the one air sound as it lifted off, it is soundless. I think it is a Boreal Owl. I will check my memory with the Cornell Bird Identification tonight before I say for sure. One of the Birds I want to see on this trip. It doesn't live in Washington. It is not endangered but only lives around the world in the Boreal Forest.

A relief upon arrival as there is no one here, also a benefit to be away from the young couples. They just ignored me, which was good, but I always prefer to not be around people who drink heavily.

Cornell says Boreal Owl —big-headed—framed with black eye disks —earless, well, not visible, just no tuffs—small but very round Crow size—yellowish bill—chocolate underneath—short tail—gentle, meaning a tame wild animal—nocturnal—far north—whistles like water dripping.

That is my Bird-- middle of the day but then it was napping I rousted it out. Didn't get to hear it whistle.

Goodnight
Edna

Bird - Boreal Owl - excited to have seen one.

Moose Lake

August 22

Hot Broth
Too Many Stars
No Moon

Dear Sister Ursula,

The portage to Larch Lake is uneventful. Dry trail, gradual low hill going up and going down. A little over a mile. I did the doubling up and made it in three trips. I am glad the campsite is only a couple of miles from here. A quick paddle to the campsite, and I set up camp and hammock. I have to do a little laundry. I decide to have boiled jerky and dried peas; I put them on to soak. The hot broth feels very comforting, and I am ready to crawl into bed. Fortunately, with a light breeze, there are no biting Bugs.

I did ten hours of paddling plus the long portage. Map says eighteen miles, and a one and three quarter mile portage. Today was a delightfully easy day. I could write more, but I want to get back to Dorothy, Katherine, Mary, and Christine—getting a man on the moon.

No moon is showing tonight, lots and lots of stars. I don't recognize any of the given names of the groups of stars. Maybe because it is so dark, I see more stars than I can see in the city, living with so much light pollution, or perhaps it is because the portion of the sky is different than at home, it shouldn't be as it is the same it is nearly the same latitude at Northern Minnesota and Northern Washington. Must be because I can see so many stars it doesn't look familiar.

Goodnight,

Edna

Moose to Larch Lake

August 23

Effortlessly plucks me
Boreal terrain
A Prayer and a Paddle

Dear Sister Ursula,

A short portages. Larch Lake is calm and alluring because of
its low floating mist. This whole Boundary Waters area is so
different because it is a small area where it has both the
coniferous of the boreal and the hardwoods of the non-perm-
frost terrain. I love this north woods with its mixture of
coniferous Pine Trees-- Tamarack, Black Spruce, Balsam Fir, and
the hardwoods-- Maple, Quaking Aspen and Birch are all mixed
in one forest. It is a unique area between the boreal and the
deciduous forest to the south. Many of the conifers look like the
short branch stubby tundra trees.

The White Pine is not from the northern group but the
southern and is vast. In contrast to the scrubby Black Spruce,
which is taking up as little air space as possible; the White Pine
has long outreaching branches embracing the openness of the
terrain.

I see four men on the beach, ready to launch as I enter the
cove, I hesitate and slow my approach. I think, shall I back up
and allow them to leave before I go to shore? They have their
life jackets on; they are ready. The wind is strong on my back,
pushing me forward, it will be difficult to turn about and leave.

This group of four men is about to enter Larch Lake as I
am pulling out. Two steadied the canoe keeping the waves from
bouncing the canoe on the ever-present boulders while another
reaches for my paddle, and yet another effortlessly plucks me up

out of the canoe and places me on the ground while the first two carry my canoe to land — all of this without a word.

As the big guy places me on the ground, he says, "Now that we have you out of the way, how about you helping us launch."

"Okay, what would you like me to do?" I respond.

"We could use a prayer and a paddle."

"I can handle that just fine," I answer.

At that, the first man stepped into the bow of his canoe, I say. "Wind and Water bless this man and keep him safe and happy," and I hand him his paddle.

When the second man enters the stern of the canoe, I say, "Sun and Rain keep this man calm and laughing," I hand him his paddle as his friends push him off the shore into the wind.

The big guy says, "This time will you help hold the canoe steady as we launch, your blessing and paddle work will also be helpful. Larry climb in."

"Clouds and Waves help this man enjoy the ride, and to remember he is here to embrace the wilderness." As the waves continue to crash against us, I hand him his paddle and grab the canoe in the center while I stand knee-deep in water as the big guy enters the stern. I pushed them off the boulders and said, "Trees, bless this big guy, so he and his friends are safe and return home to their families with wonderful memories."

As they paddled off into the wind, the big guy says, "You have mighty fine prayers, very fitting indeed. I don't know how you manage alone; even with the four of us, we need help. Thanks."

I took my time moving all my stuff over the short distance to Gabbro. Getting out of the wind is a relief. Rested before the launching onto Gabbro Lake. The shore is of small rocks and being an offshore wind as good as it gets. Now that I am back into the canoe, I am thinking about the prayers I placed on the men. I do not know how I knew what each man needed to hear, but I know that I hit it correctly, though if I look at what I said all of them would fit anyone, but I know I was inspired by their personalities even though I didn't meet them or talk to them, but still I was influenced by their energies.

The second portage was very much like the first. Well, the physical set up of the portage was very similar. Nothing else was. No four men with no on-shore wind. Just me spending time getting in and out of the canoe with all my stuff. The trail was smooth and flat. I stopped for a few minutes and enjoyed the peace and beauty of the Quaking Aspen Trees dancing in the breeze.

Just as I launched onto Tanner Lake, twenty feet from me is a Muskrat. It is difficult to see as it barely is out of the water when it is up. Then as smoothly as can be, it is gone. I sit and wait for it to come up. I almost miss it as it goes a long way, much longer underwater than the Loon, and swims much further before surfacing. Unless it is a different one, and I missed the first one altogether. The truth is, I don't know the habits of these little critters. Fun to see this little guy in the wild. Last time I saw one was in a very oily ditch in the city. I felt so sorry for that little fella. This one is in pristine water full of Fish. As far as I know, he is where he has the best life possible for a Muskrat.

As I lie here in my hammock looking at the clouds speed by, I realize I don't know the terminology for the part of the clouds. Are the little pieces of clouds liquid or vapor? Does it depend on the cloud? Hail, of course, comes as frozen round balls. I read one time what makes hail round as I did about snow being flakes, but I don't remember the explanation. Maybe they are all vapor until the vapor bits join together in a group and become heavy enough for gravity to pull them down to earth.

That is my theory. All I have to do is look it up to see if I am right when I get back to the internet, there is nothing on my computer about clouds .

Just thinking of the wonder of the internet is quite the contrast here in the woods. The fact is some scientists did experiments to discover all of this and so much more. Water sure is beautiful and excellent in all of its forms.

The sky is full of water; the lakes are water; I am a high percentage of water. The clouds against the blue sky are so very entertaining.

Ursula, I love writing to you. You are always so kind and are never bored with my thoughts.

I just had this thought as I do my closing that I have difficulty remembering to identify the plants. Maybe because they don't move, they sway in the wind, very flexible and don't show fear, run, swim or fly away whereas the animal kingdom dominates the environment when present, the plants wait.

I tried to look up a song called Trees by Rush a hard rock band, but it isn't in my computer. I must say I am not overly fond of hard rock, but this song is really funny. I cannot remember many of the words, but some of the lines are funny. "There is unrest in the forest - Trouble with the trees - The maples want more sunlight, The oaks ignore their pleas - the oaks grab up all the sunlight. The Oaks don't understand why the Maples cannot be happy in the shade. Typical oppressor. I don't remember more.
Goodnight,
Edna

Birds - Golden Eye Duck
Animal - Muskrat
Larch to Gabbro to Tanner

53

August 24

Listening to small sounds
Clear Sky
Refreshing swim

Dear Sister Ursula,

    Clear weather maybe the first day with no clouds in the sky, the reflection on the water sees double. Only the Ducks, Loons, and I make ripples on the surface of the lake. Silent. I hear my paddle splashing even when I work at making no sound; it seems noisy in this silence.

    The harder I try to paddle without a sound, the louder the dripping of the water off of the paddle seems to make. The ping-ping-ping, of the drops, intensifies in my head; it gets louder with each stroke until all I hear is the contrast of the pinging to the sound of the canoe breaking the water across its bow.

    A Duck, I think it is a Blue Teal because it is the only Duck I know that has so much blue on its wings. It lands ten yards to my right. The sound is overwhelming, startling me and making me wonder if it always makes that much noise. It is so still, not a breath of air movement. I am hot and sweaty in the noonday sun. I go to shore as soon as I find a desirable place, I need to cool down. I take a little refreshing swim rinsing out my clothes. It is essential to cool down and to get the sweat off of my skin.

    I rest and read until late afternoon; it is cooling down. I paddle and portage—only memorable thing is the abundance of Ruffed Grouse at the portage. They are such beautiful birds and cute as their head feathers standing straight up. It looks like they forgot to comb their hair when they got up.

Yup, I finished the book; 'Hidden Figures.' It is about success, change, determination, pride, self-confidence, through looking at racism and sexism. I quote what the author, Margot Shetterly, says in her notes, which says it all. "The idea that black women had been recruited to work as mathematicians at the NASA installation in the south during the days of segregation defies our expectations and challenges much of what we think we know about American history."

Goodnight,
Edna

Bird – Yup a Blue-Winged Teal, Ruffed Grouse

Tanner Lake

August 26

Miserable day
Horrible rocks
What was I thinking

Dear Sister Ursula,

Whatever possessed me to think this trip is a good idea. I am all alone, no one to blame my miserable day on but me. No one available to help. This trip is a stupid idea. There is no one else, just me. I am miserable, Sister Ursula. I am glad I didn't bring you to this wretched place. Every step is horrible rocks. Horrible soil, uninteresting rock, and more rock and more rock.

Pushing off from the beach first thing yesterday morning, I caught my left foot between two horrid rock boulders. Wrenched my left knee, tripped the canoe just enough to fill the bottom with water. If I had any sense, I would have gone to shore, but not me. I bailed the canoe and got in wet to the waist and on the right side to my armpit. The wetness doesn't matter much as it is to be sunny and will be a hot day, really hot today, and I will dry, but I am uncomfortable and miserable.

The best part of the day is that I dried off and warmed in the hot sun.

Because my knee hurt and my ankle is swelling, I didn't want to go to shore. So I paddled beyond my destination campsite, knowing the next campsite is only five more miles. Only! What was I thinking? Not thinking well, I assure you.

That is when my miserable lousy day turned worse. The wind went from gentle breeze to a strong head-on, then to a very strong a little offshore and head on strong at the eleven o'clock directional bearing.

So paddling only on the right side worked well, at least for a while, then the wind changed to ten o'clock bearing. No matter how strongly I paddled, I couldn't overcome the wind as it continued to push me away from shore.

The sun was also in my face, so I put on my cap; I had tightened my cap, but a gust of wind took my hat anyway. At the moment, my thought was I hope it landed in the canoe. No such luck today. It most likely landed in the lake a hundred feet behind the boat. Now I have three-foot waves breaking and spraying into the canoe. I cannot get close to the shore. I cannot keep up this deep hard paddling. Even the extra arch sweeping will not beat the damn wind. I stop paddling against the wind and start paddling backward as the wind turns the canoe 180 degrees. I steer the canoe towards the shore. I've lost at least a mile to get close to shore. I still want to turn into the wind and go onto the next destination.

I cannot even turn it into the wind with the shore protection, then I come close to the wind tipping the canoe, and I took on a gallon of water. I said to the wind, "Okay, I am defeated. I will not try again to turn against you, you win. You are much stronger and more persistent than I." I paddle back the three miles to the destination I had planned to reach today.

The landing beach at the campsite is a rock on rock on rock. I've been barefoot all day; fortunately, my water booties slide on without my ankle objecting. That is what I think as my knee screams in agony when I crouch to get out of the canoe. Then my ankle awakens as I put weight on it as I step on it in the attempt to lift my right leg out into the water.

My head spins in dizziness. All I see is black. I am holding onto the canoe with both hands standing in knee-deep water with the wind and waves splashing off the rocks behind me, soaking me thoroughly. I can do nothing but sit in the water, holding onto the canoe gunnel and waiting for my vision to clear.

I have had this reaction before, as you know, Sister Ursula. It is just waiting for the shock to subside. Yes, blind people manage every day, more challenging situations crossing busy streets, finding their house keys that slip out of their hands. However, I have no such sympathy at the moment. I am not afraid as I sit, struggling to keep my grip on the canoe with my exhausted arms. I know it will only take time, and my vision will come back. I know it is induced by the pain, the pain will subside, and the darkness will leave.

The moment I hear in my head, I am not afraid the fears begin to compound. I even imagine the campsite has a family of Moose awaiting to trample me as soon as I manage to get to shore. Now, I wonder why I thought the Moose would wait until I was out of the water.

My usual landing is organized, and I empty the canoe with great care to keep all my belongings dry even though they are all in dry bags and Ziplock bags inside dry bags.

Not today, everything gets flung onto the beach from the canoe as the waves continue to add water into the canoe and up over me. I heave everything as hard as I can onto the beach.

By continuing to lean heavily onto the canoe, I manage to get everything out. I can see now, though my head feels hot, a huge contrast to the rest of my body that is beginning to feel cold. I struggle to the bow and get in front of the canoe, and I perch on a pointy boulder. Not a desirable chair, but from this position, I manage to pull the canoe halfway out of the water. Crab walking using my two hands and one foot, I get the canoe completely out of the water and turn it over.

For a few moments, I panic. I cannot locate the paddle among my strewn things. I do not remember anything about any of my belongings while unloading the canoe, just the flinging of everything I could reach.

What else can happen to make this horrid day worse? Yes, I know you would know-Rain. Although you in your water world wouldn't find adding more water inconvenient, However, I am cold, and the rain is cold.

I have not been pitching the tent. Hanging the hammock has been what I have done most of the time; however, tonight, I need the larger shelter without a doubt. Hopping and crab walking around in the thunderstorm, I pitch the tent and get all my gear off the beach and to the front door of the tent. I pull up the canoe a little further from the water and tie it to a tree.

Soaked to the skin, I enter the tent. My head is no longer burning hot. I am shivering with cold, possibly pain, though I feel nothing. I know I am exhausted, but I don't feel anything. This tent was my most significant decision of the trip.

Tonight I know I made the correct decision to bring the bigger tent.

It is big enough for me, all my wet gear and space enough to take out the dry contents as needed and keep them dry on the dry side of the tent. I strip off all of my wet clothing and dump them in a pile near the door on the wet side. I lay out my pad, sleeping bag, and put on dry wool socks — one on my right foot, and the other over my left foot toes. There are so many things left to do to take care of myself. I want to sleep. I force myself to drink fourteen ounces of water before I wrap my polar fleece blanket around myself and lie down, pulling my sleeping bag over the top.

I feel panic as I awaken from my nap. I listen, it isn't raining. I know I need to drink more water and eat and see what I can do for my knee and ankle.

I start with the simplest. Food and water. Another fourteen ounces of water. It is sixteen ounces because I fill the bottle full. I choose the trail mix I made for the trip: nuts, seeds, and grain. No sugar, no salt. I also dig out the dried fruit and jerky. I decided to take two Tylenol as prevention because I want to deal with swelling. I awaken warm. I put on my Angora sweater and the lambs wool pants so I can get out of my bedding and stay warm. I am a little concerned about shock as I am feeling nothing and I am think I feel better than I know I possibly can. It isn't reasonable that I am not feeling pain.

Lying back on my warm and cozy blankets, I gently begin my knee stretches and exercises. I start by gently working my knee and messaging until it feels relaxed. Another lesson, though, I have come across this one many times before. It is essential not to skip stretching and using the knee throughout the day. My knee needs a good workout, to keep it lubricated

Another wave of the storm has come upon me. The tent is constantly plummeted with tablespoon size drops and strong wind. I feel amazingly secure and nestle into the blankets and sleep again.

Sister Ursula, I keep going on and on about the day, but it was very long and miserable. After awaking again, I gently repeat my knee stretches. I needed to go out, but it is still raining, and getting out and back in again is going to be quite the effort. My ankle is throbbing. It is time to take a good look and assess what I did to it.

A very sharp and pointed rock has pierced it right under the ankle nob. Quite certain the rock went all the way to the bone. It does not appear to be sprained or twisted. I had a similar experience when I became caught in the current of the Little Quilcene River. The river slammed my left knee into a sharp rock under the water. It didn't bleed much, but it took a while for the bone to heal. Again what I have is a deep, small gash. Feels like the bone has been damaged. I didn't notice the bleeding because it was in the water.

I have also done this behavior before when confronted with fear. Kept myself so busy I didn't have to face the possibility of it being a real injury. Momentum got me into the canoe this morning.

With a dab of Neosporin and a band-aid, I went back to sleep.

Now, Sister Ursula, it is four AM, and I am going back to sleep. Thanks for listening, my little golden friend.

I didn't notice any birds, animals, or plants. I was too miserable.

Goodnight,
Edna

Tanner Lake

August 27

Forced rest days
Birds pounding on trees
Almost forgot the Rabbits

Dear Sister Ursula,

The sun shines bright as I awake with my pen still in my hand though I did turn off the headlamp.

I somehow lost track of what day it is, I have been resting, but is it two days or one? I planned to write last night but didn't fell asleep. I know at least one full day resting and taking care of my throbbing knee and ankle. I assess my body and do my knee stretches. My knee seems okay. Looking out the tent door, Tanner Lake is flat calm. No breeze rustling the Paper Birch leaves that surround the little clearing. I drink another fourteen ounces of water with Tylenol.

Last night I convinced myself that today would be a complete rest day or was that the night before. I would also not be grumpy because I have to rest. In looking at the last thing I wrote, I saw that I missed the point of life by not noticing any of the wonders of the world. As I went off to sleep, I resolved that I would not waste another day of my life being miserable.

I stand and gently tested my left knee and ankle. Ankle hurts, but not any disability type injury. The knee is about what it usually is in the morning after a long hike the day before. Just let me know it is arthritic and needs continuous special care.

I inspect my surroundings. It is a lovely campsite; grassy flat area for the tent, with a view through the trees of the lake twenty feet away. Choices of Birch Trees that are the perfect distance apart to hang the hammock. I cannot see them, but I heard Birds pecking on a couple of dead standing trees.

I have not eaten a cooked meal for what seemed like an eternity. I cook pancakes, boil some jerky, and scramble eggs. It takes a few meals, but powdered eggs with spices taste just fine. I am making enough of everything for a cold lunch and dinner, as well. I choose a spot to hang my hammock, so I can observe the trees where the Birds are pounding on the Trees and lie down.

I realize as I recline just how tired I am — the efforts of injury and my noticing my reaction. I feel weak everywhere. My ankle is throbbing, but not an intense feeling, just a soft throb. I force myself to stretch my knees again.

With patience, I don't usually have I watch the Tree where I can see the movement behind a few branches of a large Bird, but not clearly enough to identify. Flew off and came back several times. I open my Bird identification folder to Woodpeckers. I am ready for when I get a good look. I continued to drink water, read and wait for the Bird to show itself. I see him; he has come around to my side of the Tree in an open window between branches; black spots in lines on a white body, black mask on the white face, and a brilliant red spot on its head above the eye. No question it is a Hairy Woodpecker. It is the size of a Robin, but not chubby, slim and elegant.

I almost forgot the Hare. They are in abundance; I have seen many Snowshoe Hare's. These little Rabbits have to be remembered. They are lovely and like all Rabbits trusting and afraid all at the same time. I have brought along snares in case I decide I want to eat rabbit. I do not need to eat rabbit at the moment. These little rodents have enormous ears and feet compared to their body size.

Fish are beautiful and it is easy for me to catch, clean and eat. However, snaring a Rabbit and dressing it out and eating it is more difficult. Doesn't make sense, but that is the way it is, I will only eat Rabbit if I run out of food. Being cute and adorable makes them harder to emotionally kill. They seem defenseless where a Fish is strong fighting and does not give off the delicate vibes when caught nor is it terrified. The Fish will look me in the eye with defiance and anger; not the Rabbit, it just shows fear.

Edna

Birds - Hairy Woodpecker, Kingfisher
Animal - Snowshoe Hare
Plants - Paper Birch

Tanner Lake

August 28

Knitting a code
Don Quixote
Staying Another Day

Dear Sister Ursula,

All-day, I had the feeling I need to get up out of the hammock and pack my gear and move on. The truth is I don't need to, and the effort to move will be outweighing the need, and it is wiser to stay here and enjoy this lovely spot. I contemplate starting another book. The sun is shining, and I put out the solar panel and begin to charge everything. I need to pump water today. Just the effort of getting around to keep the solar panel in the sun and doing the necessary chores is an enormous effort. But, I am so relieved; other than bruises and the little ankle cut, I am okay, nothing serious that will last. I could move on, but it is better to stay, it is too much unnecessary effort to pack up and leave.

I am glad I decided to stay the day. I turned on music, but it was irritating to me to disrupt the silence of the environment. I am thinking about starting another book. However, I don't know what I am in the mood to read. I need something that will be more interesting than looking at the leaves flutter in the wind. More captivating than pain throbbing in my ankle. I tried to read Miguel de Cervantes' "Don Quixote" a few years ago. Couldn't get into it. If I cannot pronounce the title of a book, it isn't a good start. I was assigned "A Tale of Two Cities" in high school, but I don't think I actually read it.

I only remember that there is a war in France and a woman sits in the pub knitting all the time. I had started knitting when I was eight and had made many hats, scarves, and sweaters. I was fascinated with the idea of knitting in a message. I wanted to know more about how they did the coding. The teacher wasn't interested in my questions about knitting in a message. He probably had no idea how it would be done and so belittled my question. Well, we were even, I was uninterested in reading about the war and, I told him so.

How about-- "The Little Prince"? I did read it forty years ago, but I may have been too young then. That is a possibility. The Chinese "Dream of the Red Chamber" came highly recommended. Of course, I am familiar with Pinocchio, but I have never read it. "The adventures of Pinocchio," I don't even know if the children's book is the book or if it is adapted. I think I will start with Pinocchio. I have lied to myself enough these last few days I need to check out my nose. I don't think it is any longer.

Goodnight,
Edna

Tanner

August 29

Rain
Pinocchio
Don't be lazy

Dear Sister Ursula,

Stayed, and now it is raining, and I will be here today. I could have moved on in the afternoon when it seemed like it was done raining, but decide to stay. It is so much easier to break and set up a dry camp, but if I needed to move on, I could have. I am fighting my inner voice saying, don't be lazy, get going.

Finished Pinocchio, fantastic story, completely different than the little picture book I had read to the children. A Disney book. The original books, a fictional character, a puppet named Pinocchio, the protagonist of the children's novel. I think it is written for adults entertainment trying to teach their children to have desirable behavior. Carlo Collodi is a fantastic Italian writer. It was printed in the mid-1800s. So glad I read it. Sister Ursula, you would like it as Pinocchio is a real prankster who is off having adventures, much like all boys who want to play and don't want to spend all day going to school — originally written as a series.

I need to pump water when the rain lightens. It is a cold rain. I have my warmest clothes on and my full rain suit.

I am looking forward to climbing into my sleeping bag with my polar fleece blanket. But I will wait until dark as the night gets to feeling long this time of year, about eleven hours long the end of August.

I saw a few Crows up in the Balsam tree, I don't know why, but I decided to caw-caw at them. They answered by scooping down, cawing back. I don't know what I said, but the six came in looking around. I didn't say another thing. Just watched, they eventually lost interest and left.

I put up the tarp so I will have a non-raining spot to cook. It really makes a difference; I wanted to drink hot tea and have quinoa and cooking under the tarp is most desirable even in a light drizzle.

I will limit the amount or quinoa, so it will last as quinoa is turning out to be a favorite meal on this trip; I will bring more on my next outing. I do have some chia for variety to add to the pancakes, and I still have a couple of servings of wheat berries.

After dinner, I went out in the canoe. It is still drizzling, but there is only a slight breeze desirable to be out on the water. With the Fish actively eating the Bugs off of the water top, I thought it might be possible to interest them in a Bug on a hook. They took my bait and left the hook — no Fish for tomorrow's meal.

Goodnight,
Edna

Balsam Trees
The ever-present Crows looking for a hand out. I have learned they don't get my food.

August 30

Connect With Civilization
The Out
For what are you waiting?

Dear Sister Ursula,

Good day, another sunny day, I was going to stay in this
beautiful spot another day, but with the lake so calm and only
five miles to the portage where I can camp I decided to move
on. My knee and ankle are okay. I hate movies where the hero is
beaten up, facing death, has broken ribs, scraped up face, a knife
wound in the leg. Then the next day, everything has unbelievably
healed even runs a marathon. It just isn't believable, but the fact
is I am okay. The ankle is tender, but only an injury that hurts
with every step, but nothing that would keep me from going on
with the usual activities of any day at home or work.

Sister Ursula, I am going to load up and go the five miles to
the next campsite. I have rested enough, and it is time to move. I
will write more tonight after I try for a Fish tonight.

Sister Ursula, I am back. I paddled slowly today. Arms feel
weak from the overexertion from the miserable, horrible day.
After two hours, I found a sandy beach and pulled up to make
sure I didn't mess up my knee. My knee is good. I am good as
well, and did my stretches, and I am feeling no pain. My ankle is
a bit puffy and bruised. Tender to the touch. I am very gentle
with it. I was tempted to stay at the sandy beach site. I didn't
because all the write-ups and the people I have met ask everyone
to camp only in the designated campsites. The exception is an
emergency, of which I don't qualify at the moment. I paddled
right by this spot two times the other day, and I didn't see it.

69

The food I had cooked and thought would last me a couple of days is all eaten at lunch. I ate some with peanut butter and some with coconut butter. It was a simple meal but very satisfying. It just tasted so good that I kept eating.

I am amazed at how many beautiful campsites I have found. The warming sun is relaxing, and the small gravel beach is inviting. I pull the canoe halfway out of the water. Sit down on the sandy beach and put both feet on the bow and lay back, allowing the sun to warm and relax my whole being. As I look at the sky, I enjoy the connection I have with civilization through watching a jet leave a gleaming white stream across the otherwise cloudless sky. If I didn't know it was a jet from my life experiences, I wonder what I would think it was. A being from outer space? God? The Devil? Who knows what my imagination would make of it.

Through my sleep, I hear, "Are you all right?" I open my eyes to a young sparkling eyed man. He is so cute with his dancing blue eyes and curly hair sticking out from his hat; I think I am dreaming though I read concern in his face.

I ask, "Are you one of my grandsons? What are you doing here?"

I could see that this wasn't funny to him and brings on more concern.

"I know you are not. I am not senile."

"This campsite isn't big. Do you mind sharing?"

"That would be fine, though I want the spot between those two trees.

"Are you sure, it's all brushy?" The young man says.

"Positive, I will hang my hammock there. It will be perfect." As I am putting the first load of my gear down by the trees, my unexpected guest has pulled my canoe up out of the water, grabbed an armload of my equipment, and trotted it up to me, saying, "I will bring the rest."

"Thank you. What is your name? I am Edna."

"Jamie, and you're not old enough to be my Grandmother."

"Well, yes, I am. You are under twenty-five, and I am nearly seventy. You do the math."

"Both of my Grandmothers are younger. Not really though, they are not like you."

"You just met me; my experience tells me that your grandmothers and I are most likely more alike than different."

Jamie headed off into the woods as I set up my camp. A few minutes later, he comes back and with enthusiasm, states, "You must follow this trail back a hundred feet and see the outhouse without a house."

"Later," I say. "What shall we call an outhouse without a house? Maybe an Out."

Jamie says, "Good idea, I'll cook us a main dish if you provide a dessert."

"Okay, do you have any allergies? Mine are bell peppers and dairy."

"I didn't bring the sour cream, and I have no bell peppers. I don't eat melons just in case you have any." He says with a laugh.

I made peanut butter trail mix balls for dessert and Jamie provides homemade dehydrated beef stew. "I haven't wanted to cook this because it makes so much food. It is challenging to keep when the weather is warm. The recipe is for four servings. I should have vacuum packed it in two portions. It has been too much to cook and eat alone. This is perfect; we can have the leftovers for breakfast. You have dessert? I was joking about dessert," says Jamie.

71

We sit on the gravel beach and watch the sunset over the lake. We don't say much until the Fish; big Fish start jumping. Everywhere we look, a large Fish is jumping. "That looks like at least a seven pounder." I say.

"I fished for hours yesterday and didn't get a bite figured there just wasn't any Fish in this lake."

"Jamie, what are you waiting for? It's another hour before dark.

He jumps up and is out on the water in a flash. Such excitement. Whopping and hollering with each bite. When he pulls one into the canoe, I think I will have to rescue him. Jamie's voice echo's up and down the lake. He came back with two Trout. He is managed to get in before it was too dark to see.

While Jamie was fishing, I rigged up a lift with my ropes, so we stored all our food out of reach and away from camp in case any critters decided our stew and fresh Fish was tempting.

The Out is funny. Way out here, someone put in a toilet. Dug a deep hole and put a commercial heavy plastic cone seat on a concrete pad. "Goodnight Jamie, Thanks for the dinner and everything else."

"Thanks for the dessert and the inspiration."

"Did you notice the sunset was yellow golden tonight? Not the usual Red? Or were you too busy fishing?"

"I saw the yellow on the water. I will admit I didn't focus on it."

Edna

Animal- Trout
Plants -White Pine
Tanner Lake

August 31

Can always use a tip
Aluminum banging on rocks
Beaver House

Dear Sister Ursula,

It's frustrating how I automatically change back to thinking
about others' needs so quickly. I don't know if Jamie is a light
sleeper or not. I am aware of the noises I make not wanting to
disturb his sleep.

I don't get up knowing it'll force him to start the day before
daylight. It's really okay for me to drift off again.

The tent zipper awakens me. Awe, it's morning, opening my
eyes to daylight, perfect.

"As you see, it is another perfect day in paradise," says
Jamie as he motions towards the mirror flat lake. "May I inspect
your hammock set up before you take it down?"

As I empty all of my equipment and set the gear out from
under the hammock, I say, "Sure come over. "I continue to
make up the bed, ready for inspection. I flatten out the sleeping
pad, the sleeping bag, then lift the corner so Jamie can come in
under the brown tarp.

He looks at the bedding layers, the Mosquito net, the tarp
and the parachute cords that hold it all together. "Shoes off, then
climb in and lie down, put your head over here."

"Comfy indeed. This would take some getting used to."

I pull the cord that pulls up the foot flap, and it raises so
James can see the lake, canoe and the area under the food stash.

"Now that is very convenient. I cannot count the number
of times I have gotten out of bed for a Bird or Chipmunk

checking out my presence in their home. Now I see why you wanted these two trees. A well thought out camp set up."

I told Jamie, "I've not always done this so well. This last week I've gotten a lot better. More thought has to be given to the tent set up. The hammock is easier. Trees dictate the position of the hammock, the canoe, the food stash, cannot always get them all at the foot flap."

What does his rope do?" Asks Jamie.

"Pull it gently." As he does the back rain flap lifts. Twisting awkwardly Jamie sees behind himself.

"Helpful, but it is difficult to look back."

"Yes, but easier than getting up, especially when raining, and that is why it is best to get everything at the foot."

As he gets out of my hammock, he says," Come see what I've learned.

"You're on; I can always use a tip."

Jamie has a four-season two-person tent. He takes off his outer rain fly so we can view into his tent. From front to back along the ridgeline V, he has a light cord. "Every eight inches, I have put a looped knot with a lightweight carabiner attached to each one of my important pieces of gear. At the head, I start with my pouch for my glasses; then the LED reading light holder, then a pen and pencil tube, then a flat holder for my pocket knife, then the headlamp, and last the TP. I am a bit over the top with organization, and I want to know where things are without searching through bags and around the tent floor. Explaining this to you, I feel a bit embarrassed. I feel silly."

"Oh, Jamie, it's so creative and wonderful. Sorry if I seem unimpressed. I was thinking of how I can attach something similar inside my hammock that can also be adjusted for my tent. In the morning, I am always thinking about where are my glasses and relieved when I haven't broken them in my sleep."

"You like it? As I was showing it to you, I was thinking maybe it is me just being anal," says Jamie.

"Maybe it is, but then if it appeals to us who don't like hunting through piles of stuff for our essentials. It will appeal to other people who have the same problem," I say.

"I also have a velcro pocket for my car keys. That never gets open until I get back." Jamie shows me a tiny flat pocket sewn into the inside of his life jacket."

"You could sell that idea to any-one of the many life jacket producers, or at least give it out to the world. Could save a lot of people a lot of stress." I say.

"Maybe, I will. I like sharing my abilities to design and make things," Jamie said.

Breakfast is a quick repeat of last night's stew and peanut butternut treats. We packed up our canoes.

"Did you hear the thing that went thump in the night? Sounded aluminum?" I say.

"Yes, several times," he answers.

"What do you think?"

"Maybe an aluminum canoe hitting the rocks. Where are you headed today?" he asks.

"I plan to portage the Narrows then camp at the Narrows Water Fall," I reply.

"Do you have time to spend an hour or more seeing about the aluminum sound? My guess is because the breeze is going your way; you will make good time, and the portage is short and flat. I did that portage yesterday."

"I had dismissed the sound as dreaming until you asked. It was so faint and random."

As we talk, Jamie carries all my gear and turns over the canoes placing them near the water edge readying them for filling.

"I would like to check out the cove upwind first before heading towards the Narrows. I was trying to determine the direction of the sound while listening to the aluminum thumps. The echoes on the lake make it is impossible to tell from what direction the sound was coming. Even when I stuck my head outside of the tent, I couldn't tell."

"Let's go to the cove," I say as I climb into my canoe and Jamie pushes me away from the rocks.

"It looks like a perfect spot for the wind of last night to have blown in something. With the change of wind direction, we don't hear anything. Lead us on." I say

We find nothing that looks like it could be the thumping, but there is a small stream that interests me. Perfect Moose territory. "I want to see if there is possibly a Moose in the wetlands."

"Okay with me, lead on," he answers and indicates with a dashing smile as he holds up his paddle ready.

"No Moose, but maybe we can see the Beaver that belongs to that house," Jamie says quietly.

We paddle silently to the house, and right off to the left, swimming towards us is a Beaver with a long tree limb with many branches in front of him heading for his house.

Jamie mouths, "Cool," his eyes sparkling with delight. The Beaver dives down, drawing the branch with him.

"Show is over. Where too?" I ask

"Let's follow your thinking and head towards the Narrows."

"I hope whatever it was that went thump in the night doesn't mean someone is stranded."

"Me too. That island has a camp spot, shall we cook our Fish? It is only a mile or so from here to the Narrows portage?" Jamie asks.

"What about your schedule? I ask.

"I'm having a fantastic day on the water, and it's entertaining, even saw a Black Beaver. Good company. Maybe I'll camp on the island or go back to our camp, at the moment I am still two days ahead of schedule even if I don't make any progress today," answers Jamie.

"Fish cooking it is. I have carrots we can have with the Fish."

Strangely separating and going in the opposite direction was sad for both of us. Jamie gave me his email address saying, "When your book comes out, email me so I can read about myself."

The portage was easy, reasonably smooth, and only a gradual up and down. The leftover Fish made a perfect dinner on Thelma Lake. I feel tired, I think it is mainly because my ankle is sore. I have propped it up, taken a couple of Tylenol and watching the beauty of the wind in the trees and over the water.

Edna

Animals – Black Beaver
Plants - Balsam Fir
Tanner to Thelma Lake

September 1

Welcome Visitor
Always enjoyed a lightening storm
Wolves howling

Dear Sister Ursula,

A delightful visitor today--I was deciding to stay here with my sore foot elevated on my backpack at the Narrows campsite, not breaking camp, having leftover fish for breakfast when Jamie arrives with a delightful smile.

"I was worried about you packing all your gear over the mile portage. Kept thinking you had ended up with half of your gear at Tanner Lake and the other half at Thelma. When I got to the portage, I wondered if you were over here or did something else. Glad to see you are here doing just fine without my help, sorry for the lack in trust that you are strong enough to take care of yourself."

"Good to see you. My ankle hurts, but as you see, I am okay, thanks for coming to breakfast; have some."

"I brought what I need to make pancakes; I will make enough for leftovers to use as bread for lunch and dinner."

"Sounds wonderful. I plan to spend the day here, resting and relaxing. Did you hear the Wolves last night?"

"No. I spent the night back at our camp spot. Caught two more Fish, Walleye Pike, last night--I will also cook them this morning."

"I set up my tent last night, so I could open a flap and see my canoe and food stash. Thanks for that tip. I hadn't realized how comforting it would be to be able to see my stuff at a moment's glance."

The day went by fast. Jamie went for a climb up the hillside following an animal trail looking for possible traces of Wolves. He didn't even find any scat.

I told a brief story of my life experiences and how I usually just took opportunities as they presented themselves, open for adventures. Jamie mentioned his likes and dislikes and how he is searching for what he wants to do with his life.

While we were visiting a group of six men came through. Not stopping to visit or eat, just portaged on to Tanner. Jamie decided to check on his gear left on the Tanner beach when they headed over the portage. Came back with enough of his equipment to spend the night at the campsite at the Thelma portage.

I definitely noticed the difference in my feelings of fear with the six men with Jamie here than if they had been going through with me alone.

Jamie had not cooked the Fish at breakfast, so he lit a fire and cooked the Fish as we watched the sunset over the trees. The waves were gently lapping the shore, and the breeze was picking up, bringing in large cumulous clouds.

"A little rain tonight, I should think, lightening off to the left, must be a very long way off, as I don't hear any thunder, did you?"

"Not a sound. There is some more lightning from cloud to cloud. Enticingly mesmerizing, I have always enjoyed watching a lightning storm. It gets exciting when it hits the water, sometimes bounces like skipping rocks."

Perrilee Pizzini

"I have never seen it hit the lake close by me to see it was skipping, or maybe I just never looked closely enough, I will pay more attention."

Goodnight,
Edna

Animals - Walleye Pike, Wolves Howling
Thelma Lake

September 2

Eating Bugs
Beauty remains inspiring
Geese

Dear Sister Ursula,

As we get ready for departure, I am again feeling sad to say
goodbye to Jamie. His pile of gear is ready to head back to his
canoe and head out where I have already been.

He cooks breakfast using my scrambled eggs and his
pancakes. "Are you okay to make the rest of the trip alone?"

"I'll be fine. My ankle hurts a bit, but nothing that is
disabling." We are up early to organize meals and snacks for the
day. Today I will paddle fifteen miles and two portages. Jamie
doesn't talk about his plans. We don't speak; it seems we have
said everything there is to say. I have all my things in the canoe,
and with one more hug, I climb into my canoe and announce,
"Maybe I will see a Moose today."

Jamie comes over, hugs me tightly, and gives me one of his
winning smiles and says, "Don't let the little Bugs bite."

There is no wind this morning; Bugs have found me, best to
get started. I pull up on my bug hood covering my face.

"There were no bugs last night, probably because of the
breeze." I lift my paddle in the standard canoe farewell greeting
and make my first stroke. I am looking over the water at the two
feet above the water that the Bugs are inhabiting. "With all the
bugs just above the water this morning I don't think there is a
chance of getting a Fish to bite today. The Fish are jumping and
eating. Then again I could be wrong and as they are on the

81

surface hungrily eating they might like your bate but your hook will have competition."

As I adjust my daypack and water bottle, I think about our preparation for the day. Jamie had cooked up thin pancakes for today's meals; I had made sandwiches. The bugs were flying into the almond butter and getting stuck faster than I could dig them out. I give up. I tell Jamie, "We can either eat the bugs or pick them out when eating. We have time to decide while paddling."

Jamie replies across the water, "A little free protein. I'll eat the Bugs."

The Bugs brought out the fly-catching Birds. Swallows skim the water, and the Fish are jumping. I don't think the bugs had anything to do with the enormous number of Canada Geese I see today. It must be all the young are being trained to fly as there are small and large groups of young geese practicing flying in the V formation. I am confused about the Geese. Why are there so many in one area?

The first large group exploded into action when I turned into a bay. Geese flapping, then the air was full of graceful Geese. Sister Ursula, to not bore you with the same things every day I am trying to only mention what I haven't written about before, but the Geese were a spectacular sight.

I am fighting sleep to get this entry finished. From Thelma Lake, I portaged to Four-Mile Lake then portaged into Cedar Lake, where I dug out my lunch. I had forgotten about the Bugs in the almond butter and ate two of the pancake sandwiches before I remember. I am glad I didn't remember until after I had eaten. I say out loud, "I too have eaten the bugs, Jamie," Launching on to Cedar Lake, the next campsite is five miles. I didn't want to paddle anymore. It ended up taking me twice as long than usual to go the five miles. Easy, enjoyable time gently moving along the shore. Pleasant enough, but I didn't want to be paddling. "What is going on?" I loudly say to myself.

Today was no people after I left Jamie, no animals, short trails. I am camped on Cedar Lake. So far, every day has been different and new. The beauty remains inspiring, the wilderness captivating, so what is the problem?

Goodnight,
Edna

Birds - Canada geese - an enormous number
Thelma –Fourmile Lake - Cedar

September 3

Fluttering fluff balls
Taking a break
Something sweeter

Dear Sister Ursula,

I awoke in the darkness and thought about not wanting to paddle. Cedar Lake is vast, and this campsite is perfect for spending some extended time. I will stay until I feel like paddling.

My ankle is a little swollen and is hurting with every step. Not much of a deterrent, but irritating none-the-less, not a good day to portage.

It is different this morning. I am not busy doing; sitting on a log watching the water, and the bushes are alive with tweety Birds. With my attention focused on the flittering fluff balls, I see them clearly and know many of them. Sister Ursula, I now understand why I needed to stop paddling, I need to re-establish my connection to my surroundings and not just get through them to the next stop. One of the clues is I didn't see a Bird, Plant, or Animal to write down, even though my surroundings are full of living things everywhere I choose to look. I did take note of the Geese, but there were hundreds of them flapping just feet away. Usually I see outside of myself much more than I did yesterday.

The little guys, I had heard the Winter Wren often but had not taken the time to sit and identify them. This little guy is like all Winter Wrens singing big and throwing its voice. In the same bushy area is a Ruby-Crowned Kinglet. I recognize this Bird. This Bird was the first Bird I ever identified out of a book. I had been trying for several weeks to figure out this Bird. There were many of them in the bushes around the house — very distinctive olive green coloring and white stripes on its wing and around its eye. The red on top of the head is difficult to see, and it is only on the male Birds. I don't see its red spot, or maybe this is a she and doesn't have one.

That first Bird was hard. I found a dead one in the yard, and even with it in my hand, and the book open, it was difficult, and I wasn't sure. I do give myself a little slack; later, I figured out that it was a young Bird without the mature markings.

Breakfast becomes brunch; I cook wheat berries. I have come to enjoy the taste. I brought them for the nutritional value, but they add a welcome variety. With a bit of coconut oil and I am wanting to add molasses, but I don't have any, so I settle for some raisins. It is efficient to have the same spices in everything, and I could put some in, but it just doesn't sound good tonight. It is simple, and as I usually use the same mixture of spices no matter what I cook, it has worked out ok to add out of the one Ziplock bag of spices. The variety is in where in the bag I take the spoon full of spices. Gravity continually separates the ingredients — parsley, basil, garlic, oregano rosemary, thyme, bay, and marjoram. Not tonight, I want something sweeter.

The woods have thick underbrush, hence when going for a walk means bushwhacking. I don't cut any of the bushes, push them aside, but I do want to explore the area a little and follow the Woodpecker soundings. Startled by a motion under my feet, I stop my pushing weeds of the path; a Mole scampered off of the trail, I must have terrified the little guy.

I have automatically packed my Bug jacket in my backpack as it is a light addition, and if I find I desire to wear it, it will be worth everything. I have been chewing the Plantain seeds—the weed that keeps the Mosquitoes at bay. It has been working. But tonight, I am delighted to have taken my bug suit along. Back in the woods out of the wind, there were plenty of biting Mosquitoes. I am so happy; my ankle is better tonight.

Goodnight,
Edna

Birds - Winter Wren, Ruby-Crowned Kinglet
Animals - Mole
Cedar Lake

September 4

Canoe Dock
Protected from the squall
Oil my joints

Hello Sister Ursula,

I almost go back to the beach to see what Woodpecker I
have glimpsed as I paddle out onto the lake. Luck is with me; it
flies into sight, a little guy, five to six inches with a red spot on
its' head. A Downy, they are common at the Boundary Waters
and on the west coast.

Overcast and a bit windy this morning--lightning is off to
the west sparkling from cloud to cloud. Large dark
cumulonimbus puff balls coming fast. As I skim the shore for
any place to pull up my canoe, I see there isn't any. As I look
down the beach, there are twenty-foot sheer cliffs. The other
choice is smooth round ten-foot boulders with no footholds. In
between are stones that lead to sheer cliffs. I paddle on with all
the force I have in each stroke.

The lighting clouds are getting closer. The thunder is loud; it
is too many flashes and rumbles to distinguish which flash goes
with which boom.

As I round a point of land, I see in this little bay a possible
spot about a mile to my left, which turns me into the wind. The
storm is now hitting me straight on. The canoe is creating a
spray as it hits the waves; creating a steady spray on my face. My
eyes are watering from looking directly into the strength of the
storm. The brochure indicates this part of Cedar Lake is Vale
though the map doesn't have it labeled. It's bigger than one of
the countless puddles that connect lakes; maybe it is considered

part of the Cedar Lake I just left. I think about the discrepancy as I paddle closer to shore.

The spot is looking good to pull up. No, Keep Off sign, Danger sign, Private Property sign, no dock, and no cabin. It is not exactly a beach, but it has a flat rock. I am impressed with this landing. It is how a canoe dock needs building— a flat platform three inches under the water. On the landside, it has a shelf just out of the water. I get out easily. Pull the loaded canoe up sideways onto the ledge, and I am out. Grabbing my two dry bags, I climb up a short hill into the trees. The lighting flares, and the thunderclap brings a torrent of rain before I have secured the rain tarp. I am as wet as is possible. The tarp is up, and the hammock is stretched out under the tarp. I have secured the canoe by tying both ends—one to a tree and the other to a five-foot bolder. There is no fear of a tide, but the wind and waves are a threat.

Standing under the tarp is protection from the squall. It isn't cold; I am not chilled. I change into dry clothing and lie in the hammock intrigued by the intensity of the storm. I re-plan my day. Keep dry is the top priority and rest; when this interruption from the weather passes I will continue and camp the night where I have planned. Remembering the map, I estimate that it is four more miles to the campsite.

I open my eyes as the thunder shakes the ground as if it is cheering a basketball team. It is raining hard. It has doubled in its volume. Checking the time I calculate—I landed and set the minicamp, it was mid-afternoon. Now it is after, well after the evening hour. I have been here over five hours.

I find myself laughing out loud at myself because I thought, "What shall I do?" As if there is any reasonable choice. I remember the last time I was in the rain like this; I was on the Tennessee River in Alabama. There was no choice then and there isn't any choice now. Staying out of the weather best I can is the only choice.

I am warm and dry—comfortably lying in my hammock, this rain isn't cold like it was the other day. It's raining buckets, amazingly there is a choice; I can lie here, listening to the storm or sleep.

It is dark and lightly raining when I awake. I feel a little chilly, but not cold. I dig out my headlamp and check the time —two-sixteen. Without getting out of the hammock, I wiggle into my sleeping bag. I eat a bit of trail mix. To my surprise, I sleep soundly until morning — a peaceful, unconcerned sleep.

Still raining, not as hard as last night but looks like it is settling in for an all-day rain. I mark on the map the general area where I chose to camp. I couldn't have chosen better. Even with the continuing rain, there is an excellent view of the raising-sun over the lake I will explore next. There will be a portage around the bend. I am not looking forward to the next portage. My notes say it is a rough trail. My note says 550 feet long. I will hang out here for a while and see what the weather does — deciding between reading 'The Little Prince' and 'The Color Purple.' I will put up a second tarp to cook under even if I only stay to make breakfast. I'll let you know later what I did today.

Stayed—rained and rained, and then it rained. Glad to stay here. Putting up the second tarp next to the hammock tarp worked well. I stayed dry. The trees cut down on the wind blowing through under the tarps. Pleasant and read 'The Little Prince' three times—I may read it another time, but not now the first time through I was taking the story more literally, the second time through I was getting the messages about humanity, the third time through more personal. The first time through I made a note that my lesson is—'The things that are important are the thing that are not seen." The second time through, I added, 'It is good to have had a friend!'. Third time through—the heart is thirsty!"

I made soup and tea today, then cooked the Thanksgiving dinner. Easy with hot water. Add a can of chicken, a package of instant potatoes, a box of stovetop dressing, dehydrated cranberries, and instant turkey gravy on the side. As it has continued to rain, the temperature has dropped considerably. A big dinner has hit the spot; with enough left over to have for breakfast and dinner tomorrow.

The rain has let up a bit. Adorned in my complete rain gear, I am going for a walk. I need exercise to oil my joints. There is an old overgrown trail that heads along the lake I will explore it. A variety of Ducks are in abundance out on the lake. The rain never seems to bother them.

Goodnight,
Edna

Cedar Lake

September 5

My dads' birthday
No more depressing stories
The Beet Fields

Dear Sister Ursula,

The wind is up; waves are brutal. There is a trail on the map.
I will see if I can find it and take a hike. I am so pleased; my
ankle is doing so well. I will wear my rain suit and take along my
bug suit, lunch and three jugs of water.

While walking up the trail, I remembered that it is my dad's
birthday. If he were still alive, it would be his 104th. He died
thirteen years ago. It doesn't seem that long ago. He was such a
good man: honest, loving, responsible, kind, and everyone liked
my dad, my friends wanted him for their dad. I was so lucky to
have him. I wish I could have taken another trip with him up
here.

I didn't find the trail though I hiked around the point
following the shore about ten to twenty feet away from the lake.
The animal path didn't see any track or scat, but I think it is a
Bear trail. Wolves don't make that large an opening. I did hear
some Wolves yesterday morning before I went to sleep. Forgot
to tell you about that.

Time to pick a new book. Maybe tomorrow. Listening to
sixties music tonight. Looking forward to social dancing when I
get home. Such an extreme difference from being out here.

Time to start another book, which means I have to decide
which one will meet my needs to be fun, adventurous, and not
depressing.

'Big Magic' by Elizabeth Gilbert. It could be emotionally draining with no humor. I read her 'Eat-Love-Pray.' Don't remember it at all. I do remember it was good. Whoopi Goldberg - 'Book.' She is funny, but it might be emotionally heavy. I haven't heard anything about it. Gary Paulson - my favorite author - haven't read his memoir 'The Beet Fields.' It might be tough, age sixteen, working in the beet fields. I want to see how he presents it.

The wind let up during the night, but by morning it picked up and kept gusting all day. I will stay until this front ends.

I still have plenty of power stored so that I will read Gary Paulson's memory of his sixteenth year.

I read it, an excellent book as always, but not up-lifting. Gary Paulson's life was difficult before he ran away from home, this coming of age experience was also tricky, but he learned fast. He started when he ran away from home and worked with the Mexicans in the Beet Fields in North Dakota. Another depressing book, what is it with these books, I am attracted to reading. I was so lucky my parents didn't drink, gamble, or go out looking for trouble.

He is out in the world alone for the first time, the work is hard; he learns about friendship, hunger, how to play poker, and how hitching a ride can quickly turn bad. Joins a carnival, working as a grunt. Discovering some questionable people are not honorable, and there are very kind and generous people. Glad I read it, but I need an uplifting in spirit book.

I will try Don Quixote again. Said to be one of the most significant writings of the earliest novels — 1700s. I give up. The first time I read it, I didn't understand what was happening, I still don't. A friend of mine then said, "You just are not spiritually advanced enough yet to understand the greatness of this piece." She must be right because two hours into this, I haven't a clue as to what is interesting. I give up. I'll try something else.

Goodnight,

Edna
Cedar Lake

September 6

Black Bear
Sniffing canoe
Turning over rocks

Dear Sister Ursula

Only a few sprinkles in the morning. The sky lightened, so I followed a trail about a quarter of a mile until it disappeared. I went back to my camp to find a young, probably a two-year-old Bear sniffing around my camp area. He definitely could smell my food cache hanging between two trees.

I stepped back into the woods to watch. At first, I couldn't tell if this Black Bear knew if I was there or not. He kept looking around—sniffing everything. Sniffed the hammock and backed off—just the unwashed human smells, I am guessing. The stove and cooking supplies would smell more like gas and soap than food; he wasn't interested. His mama must have a new cub this year, so she chased him away. I don't know if it is a girl or boy, looks like a boy. He looked directly at me, has his nose pointed towards me sniffing. I don't know if he could see me in the trees or not, but he could smell me.

He spends a lot of time standing under the cache, sniffing loudly, staring at the food bag, and reaching up pawing at the bag. Just an estimated guess, but I think he is about four feet tall standing and stretching towards the encased food. The bag is twice the distance from the ground as he is.

He climbs the tree closest to me but doesn't get to the rope, for a while, I envision him getting to the line and breaking the cord, which he could easily do if he yanked at it or decides to bite it. The vision of him eating my food wasn't part of my plan. I continued to watch until it started to rain, my guess three hours maybe more. My stomach started growling; my concern was the bear would hear it. He didn't look my way.

He must have given up on getting any food as he walked down to the beach and I could hear that he was rolling over rocks, I couldn't see him anymore so walked slowly around the edge of the clearing to a small clump of trees with bushes and sat in my rain gear in the rain watching him turn over rocks and eat. He is simply fascinating. He did one more sniffing session on the canoe, and then he ambled down the small beach to the woods and left.

Goodnight,
Edna

Animal - young Black Bear
Cedar Lake

September 7

Varied Weather
Rapids
No more depressing stories

Dear Sister Ursula,

Mostly everything was dry just damp; the breeze through the night had made it easy to pack up. I have one dry bag that has damp things in to dry out tonight if it isn't raining. This morning I am thinking about how I need to choose books by how they will affect my mood — no more heavy oppressive stories, no matter how good the book is.

I put on my ankle brace to ensure keeping my ankle from getting sore today. The sun was fully up when I get on with the day—I have entirely enjoyed taking my time moving about with ease and relaxation.

I beach at the trailhead and walk down to view the rapids, the portage guide mentions that when the water is high, it is possible to shoot the rapids instead of portaging. It looks like the rapids have plenty of water.

The rapids were a little exciting. I did get a bit wet. It was fun; I was surprised when my first thought was of disappointment that it wasn't longer. My next thought was, "No problem, it is warm, and the sun is shining. I will dry in no time." That thought was wrong. Threatening clouds obscure the sun. Definitely the easiest portage of the trip so far.

I find it amazing how things are not marked for potential danger in Canada, no signage warnings: Rapids Ahead, Trail

Head, Steep Hill, or Portage Trail. However, the maps are detailed, the portages identified by a dot.

Coming out onto the lake, what greets me is impressive waves. My guess is up to two and a half feet with little white curls on top. The flash and clap come together, and it begins to sprinkle large drops. Again I find myself paddling hard, but now I am pushing myself to make each stroke powerfully successful. Following the shore closely where the wind isn't so strong, and my strokes are making headway, I manage to get around the point where I am protected, and the waves are manageable.

The campsite has a family already, but I needed to land and stay the night. I am still a bit cold from the portage, but glad I ran the rapids. I warm up as soon as I change clothes.

Paddled six miles to the next campsite. Two gratifying hours on the water. Clouds rolled in looking like rain; clouds rolled out, looking like the perfect summer day. A breeze came up threatening whitecaps; the sun shined a path through the water. Lake turned into a mirror reflecting a double image of the lakeshore, a perfect jigsaw photo; thick black clouds rolled in, and a few drops encourage me to think about finding a landing spot. The wind picks up, making the water come alive. I slipped on my rain gear and all of this before my first break.

Drawing up to the shore, I assess that it is an excellent place to stop, no one at camp. Set up a hammock and extra tarp in case it decides to dump and not just be a simple shower. Glad I had put on my rain gear, I am dry. Did chores, too dark to charge batteries; decide not to wash clothes—better to have dry clothes.

Rolling over a few rocks, I gather a variety of Bugs; hoping one of them will entice a Fish to bite. Fish are feeding on the flying insects just above the water; they are not jumping— fascinating to be seeing Fish lips picking bugs off the surface.

Close to shore in this little alcove, the wind doesn't reach me, pleasant sitting fishing in the canoe.

Two hours later, I have a Fish on the line that doesn't get away. A Lake Trout, I decided to keep trying. Maybe I can get one more before I give up. I have another reddish beetle type Bug without a hard shell. Perhaps that is the desirable Bug. Caught one, maybe it will entice another. Rain is picking up, guess I am done fishing for tonight. While reeling in the line, I have a hit. I must have been pulling in the hook too slowly to attract these Lake Trout; something to remember when I Fish again. Sweet; I shall cook two fish for dinner—with the veggies I put to soaking it shall make a desirable meal.

It seems like a long time since I was lying around reading. I cannot remember what story I was in the middle of reading. Batteries are low will only use a computer to write until the compact energy storage units have a full charge.

Goodnight,
Edna

Animal – Lake Trout
Cedar to Jitterbug Lake

September 8

Wind
Happy B-Day Dana
Invisible egg beater

Morning Sister Ursula,

It is Dana's Birthday. I am so lucky to have the perfect daughter. I left a few small gifts for her wrapped and on her dresser. She will open them today. She was so delightful even through her teen years. Honest, always taking the high road. Strong in spirit, capable, believed she should know things before she had time to learn them. Even as a preschool child, she was a listener taking in everything, annualizing, coming to conclusions beyond her years. So intuitive, unfortunate in growing up with parents and grandparents who didn't listen, so she quit telling of her experiences--adventurous, making choices doing what she wanted to do. Bad things happen to good people, and she has had her share. Happy Birthday to Dana.

The wind continued throughout the day, gusty and swirling. Watching the wind chop off the curls from the top of the waves that spread the foaming water across the white water waves was captivating. It was as if a massive invisible eggbeater was mixing the water. Didn't do much today besides watch and listen to the wind shake the trees and play with the water — the first time I ever remember thinking about the wind playing.

WINDPLAYING

Wind rips through the woods
Clearing the trees of pollen,
Old limbs and leaves.

Gusts of air shake
Aspens' circular leaves
Sounding like chimes.

Waves pound on the shore
Bringing in the deep sound
Of the timpani.

Gusts of wind chop off the tops
Of waves spreading foaming water
Across the white-capped waves.

Watched and listened to the wind
Shake the trees and
Play with the water

First time ever
I thought about
The wind playing.

Goodnight,
Edna

Jitterbug Lake

September 9

Regrets
Trail-mix
Be kind to me

Dear Sister Ursula,

As I lie back against my daypack looking up at the sky through the White Pine branch with my feet on my food pack contemplating what I want for lunch, I decided I didn't want another bite of trailmix. Yesterday I had picked out all the nuts from the bag and ate them for the afternoon snack. At breakfast this morning, I ate all the craisins and apricot pieces with oatmeal. I ate the honey raspberry paste, which I will have to say was a highlight in food recently. I had a Lake Trout for dinner, and the Walleye Pike was mighty tasty only a few days ago. More fishing perhaps would help. I do have a few things left in the 'When I Need Something More' category. I have tubes of Strawberry jam, and Marmalade, and three sticks of dried pepperoni. I haven't eaten the dried peaches and pears. It is time to get out some of the treats.

I don't know where this disappointment in food has come. When home, it is in alignment with thoughts of the past. Maybe regrets about my childhood, or my failed marriage, or my other failures. Well, what is it this time? I am a runner. I do run from things instead of facing them. Usually, by keeping so busy, I don't have time to look at them.

I don't think I am running away from anything on this trip. I think this time alone in the wilderness is about having time to find something.

Regrets— as soon as I write that word, the song 'My Way' comes to mind. "Regrets, I have a few, but then again, too few to mention." Well, these last couple of decades, I will say I did it my way, but before that, not so much. It took a lot of struggle to become a person who did it my way; an amazing amount to get to the point I knew what I wanted and what I didn't.

I indeed have some regrets, but the main one is not sticking up for myself thirty years earlier. Every once in a while, I meet a kid that stands out as different, doesn't do things to just fit into the current mold. Doesn't think and say what others say. I admire their grounded-ness and their parents. Somehow the parents have given this child the freedom to develop as an individual.

Well, I guess it is about forgiving — the hordes of people I allowed to be cruel to me. I don't forgive them. That would be stupid, they were mean, self-serving to be as they were to me, but I can forgive myself. I guess that is the mantra for today.

I Deserve Kindness and I Will Be Kind To Myself.

It is time for some trail-mix without nuts, craisins, and apricots. I will have a little peanut butter mixed in today. Tonight or in the morning, I will have strawberry jam if I still feel deprived.

It came to me as I awaken from my nap under the White Pine that I am feeling most grateful to all the people who have dedicated their time to see that there are preserves like this one so people can become refreshed by just being in the woods. It is genuinely wild here—and by having people stay in designated camping areas, it lessens the impact on all of the vegetation. When I was in high school, Vice President Hubert Humphrey was able to convince President Johnson to include the Boundary Waters in the Federal Wilderness System. I remember it well because my dad was very enthusiastic about this, and this was a dinner topic throughout the many months it was in the newspaper covering the debate to the pros and cons. As a family, we only believed in the pros.

Goodnight,
Edna

Jitterbug Lake

September 10

What is wrong with Carol
Benadryl
I smell smoke

Dear Sister Ursula,

    I mark on the map the general area where I am. I couldn't
have chosen better. It has a great view of the raising-sun over
the lake I will explore next. There will be a portage around the
bend. I am not looking forward to the next portage. My notes
say it is a rough trail. The good news is it also says 175 feet long.
The sun is fully up. I eat the leftover fish dinner from last night.
Good thing it doesn't need more than my lake refrigeration. I
best get on with the day I am continuing to take my time moving
around. I didn't pump water as I will be doing a portage soon,
and I have three liters to make it the short distance of paddling
and over the portage.
    For lunch I have packed pepperoni with Wasa multi-grain
crackers, I am looking forward to this treat and some banana
slices I dried for the trip. After getting to the trailhead, I looked
at the campsite and contemplated camping here then forced
myself into portaging to the other side. I didn't want to. I again
think, what is going on that I don't want to continue, but I feel
forced to go. The trail is rough, but not difficult. Short distance,
I only need to watch my step.
    I bribed myself to get everything over to Rainy Lake by
telling myself I can set up camp and stay and not paddle
anymore today. Eat my pepperoni and crackers and read about a
Dorothy Molter a woman who moved to Knife Lake Pines
Resort in 1930 and lived there summer and winter. She was a

nurse who often took care of minor injuries of visitors to the Boundary Waters. Kept her license current by visiting her family in Chicago. On one of our trips out of Ely we stopped by her place and had her homemade root beer.

I wonder what is wrong with me? Do I need to take time for a hike? A nap? Reflection? Notice the surroundings? Do nothing? What? My knee has had plenty of stretching. What is it? I get over to Rainy Lake, and it is not a place to camp. Too much brush, no flat areas, no trees, just a great pebble beach for loading and unloading a couple of canoes. It would be tight for more than three canoes at this spot — no place to put the gear and people. Cooperation would be at the top of the learning curve here.

With that in mind, I need not go far. If a group comes, I need to move out. I stand and walk around the little landing area, exercising my knee and stretching out after the portage. A trail, well, not quite a path, but a place that has been walked on by many. Probably where people getaway in the bushes to pee. The thought almost discourages me from continuing through the brush. I keep on another thirty steps until I spot thimbleberries-I love these little berries. I remember the first one I ate. They have a velvety feel, similar to peach fuzz, but unlike peach fuzz, which stays dry, these little flat caps melt into a delicate sweetness. There are never many on a plant. They seem to spread more through the root system than by seeds.

I hear people talking, not what they say, but voices — time to get back to my canoe and paddle. I am inspired to leave.

Two women are just landing as I exit from my brushy walk, another canoe is coming, still a quarter-mile away. It is evident that something is very wrong with the woman hunched over in the front seat.

As I walk over to see what I can do to help the woman, one sitting in the back says, "Please help me. I don't know what is wrong with my sister."

I pull the bow of the canoe up onto the shore. Together we unload the woman and lie her on the ground. The women look like they are in their forties, and fit. I say, "Is she allergic to anything? What happened?"

"We were paddling, and she dropped her paddle into the water and slumped down. I managed to grab the paddle with a little effort and yelled at Carol, "'What is the matter with you? She didn't answer."

While she was talking, I started to assess-starting at the airway and pulse. She was breathing but very shallow, and her heart rate was slow. I say, "I am not a doctor, but I have some wilderness training. Do you have a first aid kit?" I could see no apparent bruises or cuts. The back of her neck was red, and she was much warmer than I. "She is trying to say something, but I don't understand, her words are garbled."

"I'll get it. What is wrong with Carol?"

"Is she diabetic" Is she taking any medication?"

I find a swollen and red area on her left arm just above the elbow. "I think she has been stung by something. Do you have an EpiPen?"

"I don't know what is in the first aid kit," She says.

They have some Benadryl tablets but no pen. "Get some water and see if Carol can swallow water if she can try to give her a pill. I'll get my EpiPen."

I go for my daypack and grab the pen out of it and my first aid kit.

"She cannot swallow; she seems not to understand or unable to figure out that she needs to take these pills."

As I inject the needle into her leg, she only moans a little and lies back.

"I don't know of anything she is allergic to. She does not have diabetes. She does have an inhaler. I will get it."

"Good, as soon as she can inhale, we will give her a dose," I say. "She seems to be breathing a little bit better. Her pulse seems stronger." I don't know if either of these is correct, but I thought it might ease both of these women's tension if they hear it. Being positive usually helps. "Please talk to Carol and reassure her that she will be just fine. Your voice will be soothing as she knows you."

The other canoe is drawing onto the shore. "Elaine, what the hell is going on?" asks a very disgruntled man.

With the sound of his voice, Carol reacts and tries to sit.

"Easy now." I quietly say to Carol.

"Who are you? Get away from my wife. Elaine, who is this person, and what has she done to Carol?"

"Carol, do you want me to leave?" I ask.

She grabs my hand and holds on.

"I will stay," I say as I hold her hand tightly, and ease her back to a lying position.

"We think Carol was stung by something and is having a reaction. She was having trouble breathing, and this woman gave her a shot of Benadryl, and now Carol is breathing better. I am looking for her inhaler, do you know where it is?"

"That will not help, that is for the swelling in her sinuses from an infection," the husband says.

"We will need it as soon as she can manage to use it, to help with the swelling," Elaine says, defiantly.

I continue to hold Carol's hand and ask the boy, who had come in with the husband, "Will you please bring me Carol's water bottle?"

Fortunately, I have a clean bandana around my neck, and I take it off and soak it with water and wash Carol's forehead and her face. As I do this, I can feel that the redness of the back of her neck has increased. I pour more water on the bandana and place it on the back of her neck.

The husband comes over and demands of me, "Who are you? Are you a doctor?"

"I am Edna. I am the person from that canoe, who happens to be here. I have wilderness survival training, and I carry a few supplies." I can tell he is stressed and frustrated at not being in control, but I don't like him.

"Bill, calm down and help me find the inhaler."

Bill yells at the boy, "Willy, where does your mother keep her inhaler?"

"Probably in her daypack. So it is handy if she needs it. The red zipper bag has her vitamins and bandaids."

I pour more water on the bandana and put it in Carol's right hand. She automatically dabs her face and places it over her lips and cheeks, and then leaves it on her forehead and eyes. She says, "Willy?"

"He is fine; he is looking for your inhaler."

"Red bag."

I am relieved she can talk, not loudly, and her voice is hoarse. "Willy is looking in your day pack for the red bag. Can you swallow some water and a Benadryl tablet?"

Both Willy and Bill come over. Willy sits next to his mother and puts his arm around her shoulders, supporting her as she tries to swallow the pills. Bill asks, "Carol, can you stand up."

I answer, "No. She shouldn't move; the exertion will not help. If you want to make her more comfortable, bring a mat to put under her. It is a possibility that the EpiPen treatment will make her hot, dizzy, weak, sweat, shake, anxious, and headache, but she is breathing better. She may not have any of these symptoms, but these are common. It should say this on the EpiPen. Several of these symptoms are also allergic reaction symptoms such as swelling, difficulty breathing, slow heart rate, dizzy, headache. You will need to take the EpiPen and the Benadryl package and the inhaler with you when you go to the hospital. Willy, will you please take notes? Write down everything that has happened up until now, and from now will be helpful when your mom gets in to see the Doctor. I will help you get it all down. She will need to do a follow up when you get back.

"Carol, how are you feeling? Is there anything you want?"

"No. Bill the sleeping mats and the pillow help. I want to sleep. I think I can now use the inhaler." Carol says in a raspy whisper.

"How are we going to get her out of here?" Asks Bill.

Elaine says, "Bill, while we sit here and monitor Carols' breathing, we will figure it out. My sister is strong and healthy; she will come through his."

I put my first aid kit back into my canoe and ask Willy to walk with me to a large rock up the path forty feet where his family can still see us, but where we can get all the facts down in the notebook, he has acquired for this purpose without bothering his mother and without the interference.

"I know you don't like my dad; he always gets so upset over everything that doesn't go perfectly. He feels responsible for everything. Thinks he should have somehow avoided anything that happens that isn't good."

"Unfortunately, that doesn't help when things go bad." How old are you? I would guess sixteen." I say.

109

"Good guess, I will be sixteen next week — the day before we are to arrive home. Now I don't know if mom getting sick will make it a faster trip or slower, or we will stay on schedule.

"Will, do you ever do any of the cooking? Let's make whatever your family was going to have for dinner. People under a lot of stress need to eat, and your mom needs nourishment. I have some Miso soup. I can boil a cup for her.

"Sure, I can do that. Aunt Elaine will let me know what I should cook. We can make my dad feel good about himself by him taking care of mom. What do you think we should do?"

"I think you should camp here tonight, or on the other side of the portage. There is a better place there to pitch the tents and is plenty of time today to move everything there set up camp and carry your mom over after dinner, and the camp is established."

Bill and Elaine had come to the same decisions. Only they didn't think about making dinner here first. They were impressed that Will stepped up and offered to cook and clean up dinner.

Bill came over to me while we were cooking dinner and said, "Thank you for your level head and help. We have decided to get out as fast as it is safe for Carol to ride in the canoe."

After dinner, before I loaded into my canoe, I asked Carol, "How are you, and what do you want me to do for you before I head out."

"Thank you; I believe I will be fine by tomorrow."

"Keep taking the Benadryl, follow the directions."

"Willy, it has been good to meet you—I appreciate your calmness through the events of the day. This is a good time for you to step up and do the chores so your mom can rest. Bring her water or tea, whatever she will drink, she will not feel like drinking. Important that she stays hydrated."

I gather my things and get into my canoe and leave. I head out. I am glad to leave the family. They are calmer and appearing to be coping with the situation. The dinner is cooked, and they have most everything carried over to Rainy Lake.

It is a bit late to be heading out. It will be dark before I reach the campsite. As I make it around many points I think maybe I missed the campsite in the near darkness. I look for anyplace that looks like a possible campsite. I smell smoke, must be people at the campsite.

Through the darkness, I see the campfire, small and inviting — not much choice but to see what is on-shore. I have enjoyed paddling in the near dark. I am too tired and it is too dark to continue. I am stressed thinking about the possibilities of what is waiting for me tonight. Coming in close to shore it is darker and getting difficult to see the shore. It would be impossible to locate the camp without the fire. Fortunately, the water is calm and no one is near the beach as I land, and no one is sitting around the fire.

I put on my headlamp and pull the canoe up onto the beach next to three canoes. I walk up near the fire, keeping the fire to my back. There are lights in two areas, and it looks like they are in their tents.

I am facing in the opposite direction from the tents and the fire. I turn on my headlamp and look around-they have food coolers on the ground near a tree. I find a place to hang my hammock near the lake where I left the canoe. I decide to unload my canoe and flip it over my belongings, except for my food bags, which I hang in a tree behind my hammock. I put my bed together, take off my clothes, and put on my sleeping shorts and a shirt. It feels good to be lying down. My pile of clothing will not reveal that I am female. I put a lot of care into how everything looks. It is impossible to tell my gear belongs to a woman. Up close, I can't disguise myself as male, but out on the water at a distance, my gear doesn't give me away. I didn't bring my favorite pink boots even though they are perfect, lightweight, comfortable to wear in the canoe, soft, and easy to pack. Way too evident that they belong to a woman. My pile of clothing under my hammock are non-gender, with these reassurances, I breathe easily.

I hear voices and sit up, picking up the side of the tarp that exposes the fire I see the outline of two men. They are murmuring. I cannot hear what they are saying. I keep myself breathing in and out slowly. Quietly I lie back down and force myself to be still and breathe slowly. They have walked down to the canoes. Not long after I hear one of the men say, "Well, we will wait until morning to greet the fellow traveler.

Goodnight, Joe, I will tend to the fire."

I have my reading light on under the covers as I write, no light is escaping my hammock haven. I have checked before, and it doesn't show unless a person is under my tarp. That would be creepy. I am also tired, it has been a long day, and I didn't sleep long last night, though I did have a restful day in the canoe. Well, until Carol showed up in my life. That was stressful.

Goodnight,
Edna

Jitterbug to Rainy Lake

September 11

Anxious to leave camp
Night Paddle
Afraid with no cause

Dear Sister Ursula,

It is quiet and still dark, but it feels like it will be morning soon. Though the moon is a sliver, it puts off enough light, even though the trees, to see the ground and obstacles to step over and around. The only human sound is coming from the tents—snoring from the men I haven't met. I wouldn't have stopped if it hadn't gotten dark before I made the last mile. I knew it was just around a few more bends along the shore. I made a good choice in staying with Carol and in leaving them. Fortunately, it is not raining, and there is only a slight breeze. I take the time to put on my ankle brace and do a few stretches before I pack my hammock and load up the canoe.

I like being on the water in the dark with streaks of moonlight across the water, rather exciting to feel part of the environment. So very peaceful, and as I paddle around the first point that puts me out of sight of last night's camp, I feel the tension leave my body that I have felt since pulling up on the occupied beach.

I stop paddling and breathe a sigh of relief, then laugh-out-loud at myself for being so afraid with no cause. I wonder if being on this trip has made me more afraid or less? What I do know is, I like it out here alone. It might be earlier than I thought, as there is still no sign of daylight. My watch is packed away in my gear safe from water and viewing. But then there are

113

only twelve hours of daylight, the autumn equinox is now, maybe next week, close enough, in the early twenties of September.

There are either swallows or bats skimming the water for Bugs, too dark to decipher. I haven't noticed many Bugs trying to bit me, but the little predators are taking advantage of the reflection of the light off of the water and mild weather to have an early breakfast, or is it a late midnight snack.

It has been another delightful day, except for the fear I bring along with me. The beauty of the early morning paddle has put me into a meditative state. I pulled up at a gravel beach for a break and had a meal of leftover Fish. I sat in the sun after washing out two pairs of socks and a couple of shirts. Hung them in the trees to dry and laid down to listen to the Birds and fell into a deep sleep. No idea how long I slept, but my clothes were nearly dry when I gathered them to move on to the portage.

Busy place, six canoes on the beach, four more in the water waiting to land, and people were coming into the clearing from the trail heavily loaded with gear — more people in one place than I have seen in a long time. I paddle on by and look for whatever there may be to see beyond this public event — marshland with Swamp Grass, Reeds, and Cattails in their full seed pod glory. Visions of the memory of brown tube-shaped seed pods spewing thousands of little feathery fluff is a memory of what spring will be like here on this swamp. Having paddled into and near many of these perfect Moose habitats, I look, but I am not anticipating that I will see a Moose, just hoping. Therefore I am not disappointed when I don't see any. It appears to be a stream flowing into the lake, must connect to another lake. No, that is foolishness, there is no lake on the map. The reeds are high above the water. I see no movement anywhere, but that doesn't mean there isn't anything there, being low on the water in a canoe it is difficult to see far into the swampy area, aah I need to call it the marshy area as it is too deep to be called a swamp. Maybe. I need to look up the difference. Doesn't matter Moose are in both swamps and marshes.

A splash brings me back to the wilderness at hand. Ducks are plentiful, I have limited abilities with remembering Ducks, but if I pay attention, I can remember these to identify later. It has a redhead with the back of head tuffs of feathers, orange bill, white body, white under chin. I have seen this duck before, but I cannot remember its name.

I paddle up the channel a couple of hundred feet, but it is too clogged with reeds to go further. Paddling backward, I again get into the open water of the lake. I am so lucky to be here in this pristine environment.

Like magic, when I returned to the portage point, the group with four canoes have moved on, and there is only one canoe with a young couple loading getting ready to launch.

She says, "Hello, muddy trail, a bit slippery in the middle. We took lighter loads through the tricky part. My name is Edith, and this is my brother Adam. We are from Saint Paul, came up for a quick five-day trip before the snow flies. We usually come in August, but Adam couldn't get away until now, almost too late, as it is heading towards the end of September when we start school again. "

Adam says, "It is best if you start talking, or she will tell you our whole life history before you get a chance to let us know a bit about you."

Sweet college students, both in the same grad school. Twins—both are going for medical research degrees, planning on working as a team finding cures.

115

Camp-spot on this side of the portage, I tell them I am thinking about camping here. Adam said, "We know it is too late to get to the official campsite, but there is a favorite spot only a mile from here we will use camp at lightly tonight. We call it camping lightly, no fire, no clearing a tent spot. Leaving it with only a few footprints. We found it on our first trip out here when we landed there to get out of a storm. It is special to us." I was think about how he seems to talk as much as she does, but she is the one with the reputation of talking a lot, where he is considered the quiet one when Edith gets my attention.

There is an official spot two to three miles from here that isn't so busy as it will be here all afternoon and evening. It is on the right and has a gravel beach. It can be seen easily coming this way but a bit difficult to see going the way you are going. You will find it just after the Slippery Creek trail that will be on your map."

I took the tip and headed out, it is still early and there is a lot of time to get to this camp. But I didn't' find it and pulled in at dusk to a non-camp spot that has been used many times before. To dark to see much tonight.

Goodnight,
Edna

Birds - Common Merganser
Rainy Lake

September 12

Wood Grass
Such a majestic bird
Heaven on earth

Sister Ursula,

I am laughing at myself as I pack up my canoe. I have
decided that I will move out of this perfect campsite where no
one can see my camp. The low hanging White Pine tree
branches and the bushes completely hide the canoe. The
openness of the campsite is slightly away from the lake, allowing
me to see out through gaps without passers-by seeing my camp.
It is not a camp-spot, so no one is likely to stop here. But here I
am, packing and moving to a designated camp spot because it is
the rules.

I have entirely enjoyed that day of rest at the non-campsite,
will paddle the mile, and set up camp again. I only hope no one
is there. It is comforting to know I can come back here if I need
to.

I have decided to stay here for lunch. I have put out my
fishing pole, but there are no jumping Fish and no bites. I have
been thinking about Jamie and wondering more about his life.
He said he didn't date much because mostly it felt like the
women he met wanted too much too fast. Girls have asked him
out all his life, but they wanted to do movies, dinner, nothing
that is more fun to do with them than alone; they didn't add to
the enjoyment. He stayed and worked on the farm for his uncle.
His girlfriend was a senior who was fun, included him in her life.
They did things together, went to museums, collect and

categorize and mounted Bugs for her science project. Jamie said, "At first it irritated her that I called them Bugs and not by their names. She wanted me to at least give them the courtesy of calling them Insects." Jamie had paused than and looked at me and said, "You see the humor in all of this, "I laughed so hard at the intensity of her love for these Bugs and couldn't stop. Her parents came to the dining room from the kitchen to see what was happening. It was the fact that I couldn't stop laughing that won over her parents. The more my girlfriend explained to her parents, and the more she complained, the harder I laughed. Then her mother started laughing, then her father. It ended with her parents being inclusive towards me. Then as she stood there looking at the three of us laughing, she joined in the humor saying "it is just ridiculous, isn't it?"

He spent time there often, playing board games, shooting hoops with the dad and brother. It is interesting to me how similar I have been thinking that the men I meet are like the girls he is talking about, except for this one.

When she went off to college, and he started his traveling, they agreed to meet up in four years at her parents' home to see if they still wanted to be together. She wants to be a entomologist researcher. Jamie doesn't know what he wants to do, but I can see him totally supporting her in her passion with insects.

I don't know if Jamie learned from his relationship, but I certainly heard it loud and clear, "Don't settle for less than someone who will add positively to life's experience."

Maybe that is why I enjoy partner dancing. If the lead can lead, there is a real connection. Floating to the music feeling each other's movements in harmony is genuinely delightful.

Dancing, singing along and laughing in delight at the intricate moves made together is heavenly at times, even spiritual.

A Hawk flies over, leaving a little shadow on the ground. It's gray. Hmmm, the Hawk gives me an exciting feeling here in the trees, knowing that all is well and good. It is encouraging every time I see wildlife. Bears, Birds, and Plantago, or are they Plantain seeds, heaven on earth.

People were at this campsite sometime today, but gone when I arrived. They had a fire, and the embers were still warm. I brought it back to life with some twigs scattered around the fire pit and cleaned up the campsite of wood chips and twigs that had been abandoned around the clearing — burned charred wood that was left around from old fires. It looks cleaner, and I am pleased with the results. This is the first campsite on this trip where there was so much visible presence left by humans. I made a broom from some tall grasses, as a child, we call this grass "Wood Grass." I am not sure if that is correct or not; I have not spent much time identifying plants, especially grasses. I swept around the campfire, getting all the ash and twigs back into the fire pit. A good job, maybe it will help people be neater.

Quite a let down from the pristine spots I have had through the trip and it is the most heavily used of all. Quit the contrast from the one I left a couple of hours ago. This campsite isn't as lovely as the non-campsite, but I am feeling pleased to have been here. I will leave here in the morning.

The computer is charged. Lying in my hammock looking at the sky I see a group of Great Blue Herons fly over. Such a majestic birds. I love the idea of them using their feet as rudders as they fly. The first time I recognized that the extension behind the tail was their feet; I laughed at my ignorance. For years I didn't understand what made their tail look like that as I didn't see it when they were on the ground. My mind's interpretation of what my eyes had seen was a bizarre trick on me.

Continue reading 'The Elephant Whisper' by Lawrence Anthony; I fell asleep after a chapter or two, I think I will like it, doesn't seem depressing, not yet anyway. Certainly not boring. I am completely enthralled.

Goodnight,
Edna

Plant - Wood Grass - Plantain
Rainy Lake

September 13

Great Blue Heron
Ruling out Elephants
Fast and formidable

Dear Sister Ursula,

Paddling along the shore, I thought I saw some movement in the trees close to the waterline. Pulled closer to look. I saw it again, blending in well, it is more the trees are moving than I can see anything. Whatever it is, it must be larger than a person; my mind races is it a Bear, Moose, Elephant. Not an Elephant, it must be the book that brought that thought into my mind. I will rule out the possibility of an Elephant. By the height of the movement among the leaves, it is probably a Moose. One of the amazing things is how they camouflage with the environment. This huge majestic animal is blending into the foliage, the harder I look, the less I see. He must be right there, twenty feet away eating twigs, but I cannot see him just the tree rustling a little.

While watching a Moose in a swamp near Eagle River Alaska, I was amazed at how long the Moose could have its' head underwater collecting grasses. Then it would come up with a mouth full of greens spilling over. They look so cumbersome, but seeing a Moose run changes the appearance to graceful, muscular movements, like a ballet. Like the Bear and her cub, I fear to get close to a Moose calf. With that thought, I back away from the shore another ten feet. I don't see any antlers, and I certainly don't want to be trying to outrun a cow, thinking I am to close to her baby. Like the Bear, they are fast and formidable.

I decided to sit awhile and have a bit of lunch while I wait for the Moose to come into view. Sitting here having a peanut butter pancake rollup drinking cold tea is as pleasant as it gets. What I thought was a Moose silently leaves. I didn't see anything, but the tree leaves are moving a little further away. Maybe it was the smell of peanut butter that scared the Moose away; they have a keen sense of smell. I really don't believe anything I do influences what either a Bear or a Moose does, unless I irritate them. Except if I were to leave food out, the Bear would devour whatever I offered and be looking for more. That is a scary thought. An almost sighting, going to Northern Minnesota Boundary Waters and not seeing a Moose is like going to Africa and not seeing an Elephant. I also did that.

My mind wanders to when I had a job installing a photovoltaic unit at a school in Uganda on an island in Lake Victoria. On the way, I spent a couple of days sightseeing in Kenya and went on two, one-day safari trips. Both guides assured me that they always see Elephants, but I didn't see any Elephants. Nor did anyone else in our two days of exploring. A lot of Lions, Giraffes, Wildebeests, Zebras, Gorillas, and Monkeys, and I almost forgot—Cheetahs. Amazing experience. The whole time in Africa was exotic. A fantastic opportunity to see a little bit more of the world. I, without a doubt, would like to see more of Africa and it's wild animals. I may go to the reserve in South Africa where Lawrence Anthony has his reserve of wild animals. That would be an awesome experience. The book says that they have gusts staying with them to help pay for the care of all these animals. White Rhino's and Elephants, perfect adventure. He and his wife are an amazing couple. They have and will continue to move mountains to take care to preserve these wild animals

Interestingly, many of the largest mammals are herbivorous. I have never seen a Moose and a Bear in a race, but it is said that the Moose can outrun and out-swim a grizzly. Speed and endurance, scary— they can swim more than twice as fast as I can paddle and longer than I can without resting. If either of these animals is interested in catching a human, there is very little chance a person can get away just by running; there is no comparison. I can only go three miles an hour compared with them at thirty-five miles an hour, and they can run and swim for hours.

Two canoes come around the point as I head towards the bay with the trail to Marsh Lake. Friendly group, two couples, the woman in the front of the first canoe says, "Easy walk, and short, no one around, have fun."

I being in the mood to chat, answered, "Thank you, beautiful day to be on the water."

Sandy beach, footprints in the sand, but other than that untainted. Yes, smooth and uneventful portage.

Saw a siege of Sandhill Cranes again; maybe not surprising as this is the breeding ground for so many Birds. Six of them in the air earlier—I cannot count them as they are in the tall grass but looks like at least five feedings on the seeds, or they could be hunting Voles, just seeing the top of their heads occasionally. They stay in families, so this is most likely a pair with their young, as was the group this morning- the Great Blue Heron is one of the species that mate for life. And like many animals, they split from last spring's young when it is time for the next cycle of babies.

Goodnight,

Edna

Great Blue Heron
Rainy Lake to Marsh
Sandhill Cranes

September 14

Lucille Ball
Rain Storm
Under tarps

Dear Sister Ursula,

It rained so hard last night it awakened me several times. I am impressed with my tarps; they are dry, and it is warm in my hammock. The wind came up and soaked everything under my tarp, but everything is put away and buttoned-down, resulting in no problems.

Stayed all-day and read, finished the fantastic Elephant Whisper. So amazing—started. 'The Color Purple'— My first Alice Walker book—I had read it back in the mid-eighties, but I am different now than I was then. Much more aware of segregation and black oppression. Amazingly brutal book. Not a good read for me—too depressing and horrid. I almost quit reading it several times. Well, did stop reading it, changed to 'I Love Lucy' by Lucille Ball. A much better choice. What an amazing woman, ahead of her time. Demanded in the '50s to be treated better than a second-class person. Glad I had her as a role model during my teen years.

I couldn't enjoy Lucy, I had to go back and do a wrap up so I could put the story behind. Went back to the depressing 'The Color Purple' and skipped to the end where she learns her father did not kill her children. About as good as the book gets is that her children were not killed by her father. I don't need to hear about the abuse I know it exists still in many homes across our nation and the world. Blacks and Natives have been and are still abused.

I will think about the humorous choices we have in life. Yes, a redhead has it easier than a black woman. The women working for NASA as computers didn't have it easy, but the writing wasn't so impossible to read. It is a battle for all of us who fit into any oppressive category. Right now, I feel less afraid of being alone facing the challenges than I did.

It is still raining. I think I will focus on the joy I Love Lucy has brought to the people who adored her.

Goodnight,
Edna

Marsh Lake

September 15

Midwest accent
Still Raining
Wisconsin Couples

Dear Sister Ursula,

The campsite is comfortable; to keep things dry, I put up
the tent and another tarp along two sides breaking the wind and
rain. Kept the tarp down two inches to allow a draft blowing the
campfire smoke out toward the lake. Working well, however, it
drew in a couple of canoes, two married couples in their forties.
It is dumping buckets of rain.

The people coming ashore are couples, so I call out, "You
are welcome to come under my tarps and around the fire until
the rain lets up."

"Hi, I am Adam we are all from Wisconsin, born raised and
still there. We take a canoe trip every year. The four of us come
every year; we have for the last fifteen years. We come after the
summer crowds are over, and the children are back in school."

"Hello, all of our children are now old enough to leave at
home alone; in fact, only my youngest, who is sixteen, needs to
not to be home alone. She is staying with her grandparents, my
in-laws. She loves this time with them because then she can be
spoiled and they give her lots of attention, take her clothes
shopping, and she has her girlfriends over for the weekend it is
one big sleep-over for the six girls. A highlight for all of them.
I'm Mary."

"I'm Ruth. It has, of course, changed over the years as the
children grew, and their needs change, but our husbands' parents
are amazing and have made it work better than anyone could

hope. We have an agreement that we will not talk about the children while on the trip. So someone needs to change the subject."

"Joe, here I will take the bait—Thank you for sharing your fire, we were feeling a little chilled getting here. How long have you been here, paddling?"

"August 6 was the beginning of my trip," I answer.

"Wow, you have been here six weeks. That is our dream, to be out here for two months."

"Well, I will be here a little under two months. Not sure when I will end, but probably only twelve more days. I plan to take the bus to Virginia on a Wednesday; the bus only comes once a week. So I will need to get in on Tuesday to get it all together to take the morning bus on Wednesday. All that depends on the weather, my motivation, what animals I happen upon."

"Where are you from, you're speech implies, not from Wisconsin or Minnesota."

I put on my Minnesota accent and say, "Vell, yah sure you betcha, I grew up in Dulut, but I moved to dee vest coast many years ago."

Everyone laughed, and Joe says, "I believe dat es true. Vee don't talk like dat nomore, only dee old folks do."

"Yahah"

Mary says, "You have lost all of your accent."

"No, not all of it, occasionally someone from the west coast will ask me from where I come, picking up a bit of my form of speech from what or how I say it." I drop my accent and finish, "I have lived in Washington State for so many years, it has subsided. Television and rapid communications have done it to all of us—kind of a shame."

"If it isn't too personal a question, how is it you are alone out here," asks Mary.

"It is my preferred way to be with nature. It is a real treat to be alone to think, breath, and to be."

"Aren't you afraid?"

"Occasionally, but not often," I surprised myself that I was so honest.

Joe says," We have invaded long enough, the rain is almost over, we need to set up our camp."

Sitting on my little folding chair, moving the wood around to bank the fire, so it burns slowly, I open my computer and look for the next book to read.

Goodnight,
Edna

Marsh Lake

September 16,

Bats
Catch the insects in their cupped tail
Five Handed Pinochle

Dear Sister Ursula,

With the cloud cover, my batteries are charging slowly, so I am saving the power I have for writing and not reading or listening to music. Except, I opened my computer and looked up in my downloads Bats, when I saw two Bats hanging under my tarp this morning right next to the tree. They are so tiny. I have a Bat house on the side of my house, encouraging them to eat the few Mosquitoes we have around. I just looked it up on my computer, and there are three common Bats who live in the forest here. The Silver-haired Bat is a forest dweller that usually lives near water. It feeds among the trees, much like the Eastern Red Bat, though the latter is noted for its unusual feeding habits. Often a Red Bat pair will fly the same route, over and over, in search of food. Interesting, but these are not flying around eating, they are hanging out waiting for the rain to stop. Another woodland species is the Hoary Bat. It is the largest Minnesota Bat, weighing an ounce or more. All four species are solitary, roost in trees, and migrate south for the winter. Smart bats, leaving this north woods for the winter. Winters are long and cold.

Looking at the Bat, looking at the picture; I have no idea which one it is. It is a little dark under the tarp to see identifying markings. Even shining the flashlight on them, they look like hanging Bats. I must have put my rope and tarp where they usually enter under the bark of this tree. No, that cannot be right, as this tree is a birch and healthy, no loose bark on this tree.

I have never heard of Bats getting out of the rain under tarps near people. Though, I have been quite motionless in my hammock. Seeking shelter out of the rain; Bat behavior.

Fascinating tidbit of information — Insectivorous, feed mostly on flying insects. They catch the insects in their cupped tail membranes as they fly. Then as they fly, move it to their mouth. So much to know about the animals we live near.

I had to climb out of my hammock to tend to the fire. Bats didn't seem to be bothered by my movements. Heated some water and made a cup of miso soup, added the rehydrated veggies. Good light dinner. Peanut butter with trail-mix for dessert.

Stopped raining, and the neighbors came out of their tents and invited me over for roasted canned meat over the fire. I have never done that, so of course, I went. Their method worked well. They took a green tree branch split the end, wedged the meat into the split, and it held well. The canned spam sizzled and browned, it was crispy on the outside, quite good, and fun.

They play a pinochle game that is everyone for themselves, no partners, and can be played with any number of people. Worked well for five of us to play. I did get lucky and won some of the time — totally different bidding game, and since there are no partners feeding points, it is difficult to make a bid. It seems more like everyone is trying to set whoever gets the bid, instead of just trying to get as many points as possible. Somewhat like three-handed, but with so few cards, it is very different. I thoroughly enjoyed learning a new way to play a card game I know reasonably well.

I got a kick out of them talking about their children all the time, not even knowing they were. It is such a part of their lives. They live on the same block, their children go to school and socialize together, have meals together, celebrate birthdays, holidays, and do sports together. They have an open-door policy; everyone comes and goes at will. They thought about getting a house together, but decided not to, because it is working so well as it is they didn't want to make any changes.

Ruth said, "Kitchenware and garage tools are so mixed it is difficult to know who's is who's, except for family heirlooms. I learned my lesson on that when I took a platter from Mary's cabinet over the refrigerator; it was perfect for a cookie display that I used for a children's party."

Mary said, "That is why it is over the refrigerator and difficult to get, I don't want it used except for special adult occasions. It was my great grandmothers' pride and joy, as it is mine. Though I only use it occasionally, she used it daily."

They both laugh and hug, and tears roll down Mary's cheek. I am not sure why Mary is crying—she misses her great-grandmother, glad the platter didn't get broken, or is it about the fact that their friendship made it through the ordeal of her hurt and fury over a platter? Maybe a mixture of all the above.

I thought about telling them about the bats but decided not to, as so many people are afraid of bats. I know some bats carry rabies; perhaps that is why. I believe it is an irrational fear.

Goodnight,
Edna

Marsh Lake

September 17

Glean the wood
Still raining
Wisconsin Couples

Dear Sister Ursula,

It drizzled off and on all day. It would clear up, and I would
begin to pack and head out; the black clouds would roll into
view, and start to rain, then it would clear up, and the sun would
spread a few rays onto the water. Over and over, it would tease.

I put my rain gear on and went out fishing. Not sure what it
is, but the fish has armor type scales and a large mouth, quite
sure it is a Bass, but I don't know the difference between any of
these Fish. It doesn't matter as it is an open season on all fish.

I baked the Fish over the coals. I gutted it but left the head,
tail, and fins intact. Turned out perfect, moist, flaky, and tender.
I like my fish cooked beyond the recipe's recommendation of
perfection. Super-meal.

The Wisconsin couples packed up during one of the times it
quit raining, loaded the canoes, and pushed off. At that moment
the sky released the water it had been holding, they came back to
shore. I yelled for them to go to my shelter. They had rain gear
on but enjoyed being under the tarp. The deluge of rain was
flooding the entire camp.

Joe and Adam were restless, pacing around under the tarps
with the five of us—Ruth spoke to them as if they were her
teenage children and said, "Get out, go do something, leave; I
cannot stand having you two underfoot another moment." Both
men laughed and left.

"Thanks, Ruth," said Mary, "I was about to say something that I would regret."

"They will be back in about five minutes, asking if they should repack the canoes or pitch the tents," said Ruth. "Edna, what shall we tell them?"

My reply, "It is simple, what do you want to do, it doesn't have to be the right decision, just what you want to do. It'll rain or not either way."

Ruth and Mary look at each other and say at the same time, "Paddle."

We look out at the men standing next to the canoes wondering what to do. Mary says to the guys, "Paddle." It is only drizzling, the guys bail out the canoes, and in minutes we say our goodbyes, and they push off again in high spirits, laughing and splashing each other as they head out onto the lake.

I go over and glean the wood they had hauled in for their fire. Plenty to last me the afternoon and evening. The bats are still hanging in the corner. I sit and watch the bats sleep, poke at the fire to keep it just burning, and watch the rain making raindrop patterns on the lake. A little breeze has come up so that the lake has tiny ripples mixing in with the expanding circles. It would make a beautiful quilt pattern, one I will never make, but I can see it clearly on how to do it. If I were to make it, it would be outstanding.

Goodnight,
Edna

Marsh Lake

September 18

Sunshine
V formation flying south
Waterfall

Dear Sister Ursula,

Birds are singing; the sun is shining on the lake; the steam is rising off of the ground everywhere the sun reaches. I layout the solar panel and plug in the batteries—put all the wet bags into the sun, hung the damp clothing on tree branches and bushes Go back and adjust the solar panel to catch the strongest rays, turn over everything to dry the underside quicker. Decide only to pump enough water for the day, but to pack things as they dry. I think about the day ahead, anxious to get out and paddle the eight miles to the portage, then walking over to Lake Acorn. My notes say it is a nine hundred foot portage with only a fifty-foot rise with a natural slope up and then down. The trail can be boggy after rain. It'll be boggy though I am not sure what that means. Boots most likely.

Breakfast is a cooked omelet with turkey jerky and dried mushrooms. Before I eat, I move everything again—the third move so far in an attempt to follow the sun patches across the open area. Most things are dry, batteries charge slowly. The mushrooms are yummy; I had used Mushrooms with one of the meals in the first few days, but haven't since because they didn't make a favorable impression on me. I had thought that was a waste of time drying and bring these. Well, my expectations of food have changed as they were a very desirable addition to the meal.

The last thing to do is to take down the tarp where the bats are hanging. Everything else is packed and in the canoe. I look to see them one more time—they have left the protection of the tarp and are out foraging for breakfast. I had no idea when they went, but they were there when I first viewed this morning and when I took down the hammock. They were good roommates. Glad I don't have to disturb them to take my tarp.

It is good to be on the water; it seems like a long time hanging out in the rain. According to the map, there is a trail leading to a lookout about halfway to the portage. Maybe I will explore it if I can find the trailhead. There is to be a sheer cliff just before the point where the trail starts. Says there is sometimes a waterfall after it rains. That will be just the thing to do with the pleasant weather today. I took a long time leaving this morning between drying everything, pumping water, cooking, packing, and cleaning the camp of all evidence of me being there for days. It just took a lot of time. I am guessing that about the time the sun is straight up; I should see the cliff with the falls.

I am amazed at how many hills I see with rocks showing, and just before a point. When the sun reaches straight up there are no hills in sight, maybe the last place was it, but then I will keep going towards today's destination. The sun was well into the afternoon sky when I see a cliff with a waterfall. It is significant and lovely. I pull up for a stretch and a look. Grab my backpack, tie on the photocell charger, and head up the trail to the waterfall. The trail follows parallel to the creek, sometimes veering into the swampy edges. I stop at the side of the stream and wash my face and arms to cool down from the climb in today's heat. Reaching the bottom of the falls, I notice I don't have my sunglasses, so I head back down the trail to find the spot I took the prescription glasses off while I cooled down in the shade and washed in the stream. Looked at every place going down the hill and then again going up to the bottom of the waterfall. I couldn't say for sure which spot I had visited as they all looked so much the same— there went my sunglasses.

There was an amazing amount of water pouring over the edge, splashing on an area of Mossy borders, causing a thick misty atmosphere belonging in a scene of the Hobbit with Fairies and Elves. Fair waterfall, guessing twenty-five feet high and ten feet wide, tiered and split water flowing in quadruple drops over several sections of the falls. I looked again on the way back for my sunglasses; no luck.

Portage was simple, with no people, no problems. The campsite was only another three miles, uneventful. The sky is full of Ducks and Geese in V formation flying south— sometimes heading east, sometimes west, but eventually, they are going south. It is time.

The Bats as small as they are must be heading south as well, but they are invisible to me. Maybe they fly at night. In warm climates, Bats hibernate, here in Canada and Northern Minnesota it isn't possible, winters are too long and too cold.

My batteries are low; the sunshine today did get me through this evening. Hopefully, it will be sunny tomorrow, as well.

Goodnight,
Edna
Marsh Lake to Lake Acorn

September 19

Resin Oil
What is a sawbill
Swampy portage

Dear Sister Ursula,

The sun is shining, yes, my rustic living with a photocell charging requires the sun to shine—what about that for irony. I have read several books, but not listened to books or music; too noisy in this unblemished environment. I enjoy being able to use the computer to type my letters to you, Sister Ursula, and to look up things and read books. Overall it has been beneficial.

Desirable weather all day today, it was a relaxed paddle to Sawbill Lake portage. Very short portage one hundred and fifty feet, and it was flat a bit swampy in a couple of places. No people on either end. I pumped water out of a little creek flowing into Sawbill Lake. What in the world is a Sawbill? My battery is too low for using to look up things; I will have to do that later when I have more battery power.

Camp-spot is a functional, beautiful open area for drying clothes, warming in the sun, charging batteries. It has cooled down quite a bit. Glad I have my wool sweater and leggings as it is in the low forties at night. The day is okay, still getting up into the low sixties.

It feels desirable to be in the sunshine.

Pitched the tent because the trees are Balsam that has blisters that ooze an oil resin. Beautiful trees, but it is nearly impossible to get rid of the sticky oil once it is on anything. The area smells like December. They make the best trees to bring into the house with their dark green needles, smells lovely, and holds fresh for weeks.

Dinner is quick and straightforward, quinoa, rehydrated peas, and a big spoon full of spices. A satisfying meal, cooked enough for a cold meal tomorrow. Breakfast, Lunch, or Dinner doesn't matter, but enough for one of the meals when I am hungry.

With a couple of hours before dark, I decide to walk around the area to see if I can locate any of the Birds I hear. They seem to be hiding in the bushes. Looking for the Birds on the trees, I remember how we as children would poke the blisters on the balsam trees so the resin would seep down the tree trunk. The birds will eat the resin—perhaps tomorrow I will be able to see some birds from my tent before I get up.

Goodnight,
Edna

Lake Acorn to Sawbill Lake

September 20

Chickadees
Scavenger hunt
Gaggle of kids

Dear Sister Ursula

It worked, the five trees that I poked open the resin bumps have birds eating. A whole flock of Chickadees have arrived and are feasting. I hear them singing, and they are walking up and down the trunk, pecking away at the resin. So fun—I don't want to scare them away, so I stay in the tent and peek out the front door. I had no idea that it would work so well, so quickly. I am interfering with the food supply.

When we were kids, we would smash open hundreds of bubbles on the Balsam trees, just because it was so much fun, not all on one or two trees, but as we played and ran through the woods playing tag, hide and seek, scavenger hunts. Our scavenger hunts were different; they were spontaneous, started as we were sent on an errand over to neighbors to either deliver or retrieve something one of the parents wanted. It could be today's fresh milk or butter, or an invitation for dinner, or ask to pick a bushel of apples from their pie tree. One time while Lanny and I were carrying a bushel of green beans that we had picked that morning, I tripped, and the basket went flying up in the air. First, we laughed and thought it was amusing, then what happened was we needed to pick up all the beans and ended up cleaning them at the water pump before bringing them into the house.

Usually, there was a gaggle of kids, and someone would say let's find a Maple leaf or something when there were only evergreens to be seen. Whoever found the first Maple leaf would then choose the next thing to see and on it would go.

We would see the birds eating the oil, but I have no memory of them arriving so soon after the resin oozed down the tree trunks, but then we were noisy, active children running through the woods, scaring away everything.

I moved slowly around the camp, and the little Birds stayed, flew to the brush, and then back to the treat. I am tempted to taste the resin, but I am not curious enough to take the chance of a stomach ache.

I have been in a different mood today, maybe nostalgic, thinking about my freedom in the woods as a child and seeing wild animals—Ants, Fireflies, Crickets, Chipmunks, Squirrels, Frogs, Turtles, Water Skippers, Deer, and occasionally a Black Bear, Beavers, Birds, Ducks, of course Ticks and the biting Insects. I loved watching the Honey Bees. When my aunt would care for the hives I had to stay ten feet away, she would wear a screened bee bonnet so the Bees couldn't land on her face, a long sleeve shirt, but no gloves and Bees would swarm around her; she checked for problems and took out some of the full racks of honey. Ten feet away, I would sit in the field and watch; occasionally, she would ask me to haul the wagon that was full of honey over to the truck and bring back an empty rack box. Bees follow either on the cart with the honey or in the air flying around the honey and me. My aunty taught me not to swat or yell or run or be afraid that the bees were just concerned and wanted to see what was happening. It worked, as I never was stung, nor was I fearful of Honey Bees. However Wasps, Yellow

Jackets, and Hornets are a different matter. They are mean and unpredictable, I hear this in my head, and it sounds like me when I was nine, and I was stung several times and was very cross, as I didn't do anything to them and they attacked me. I can even feel my lip in a pout that I exhibited when I was nine.

Portage was simple, actually not a portage, but a very narrow water path between the two lakes. Tree limbs touching overhead as I glide under the arches. Grasses were filling the area from shore to shore. As I paddle, I hit bottom, often even with the paddle only halfway into the water. I don't scrape the bottom, but with two people in the canoe with the added gear, it would likely mean polling part of the time. The water trail was seen because of the constant flow, marking a trail in the water. The notes say it is a quarter-mile, but it seems longer as I linger looking at the Lilly pads. Not a bloom in view, but some old pods visible.

Leaving Sawbill Lake behind, I looked up the meaning. A Sawbill has two definitions: a list given to a sawyer of sizes to saw from logs, and a Bird with a jagged bill, rather like a saw blade. The next time I see a merganser, I will have to check out its bill. Probably cannot see it unless it has its mouth open. Merriam-Webster didn't say.

Gossip Lake's edges are all swamp, with tall grass coming into the lake twenty to fifty feet everywhere—even at the portage and camp spots, I think the canoes coming and going have kept the grass down for a few feet, making a trail out to the open water. It is calm, clear weather, no waves, no clouds. Warm this evening, but as soon as the sun dropped behind the trees, the warmth went with it. It is so quiet here tonight. No wind or water sounds, as I lay in my hammock listening, I can hear my breath. The sound of a Woodpecker breaks the silence as it beats on a tree. Then silence again with a hint of the sound I get when

141

I put a large conch to my ear. The sea, incidentally, there are none closer than 1,500 miles, only the roar in my head.

I get up, take my binoculars and look for the Woodpecker, no luck as the reverberating sound of echoing across the lake. I sit and listen with my eyes closed. A beautiful sound, it's methodical, rhythmical, and enticing. If it were spring I would think he was calling his mate.

Goodnight,
Edna

Sawbill Lake to Gossip Lake

September 21

Moose decline
Great Blue Heron
Too beautiful to leave

Dear Sister Ursula,

   The first campsite was only an hour paddle from the portage. No canoes at the pull-up so decided to land and take a look around, again it had a narrow trail through the water grasses and reeds made by paddles coming ashore. Swampy, muddy landing—but the ground a mere three feet from the water is dry and clean. I decide to stay before I even walk the twenty feet up to the campsite.

   I cannot say for sure, but it looks like a Moose trail along the lakes edge, with a little imagination I can see a large animal hidden in the grasses moving along munching on the delicious tender chutes from the bottom of the marshlands. No head or antlers come up above the top of the greenery. The number of Moose is dwindling here in Canada as they are in many areas of the US, including Alaska. There seem to be many reasons— diseases mostly, brainworm, a winter tick infestation, bacterial infections from injuries, and liver flukes. Climate change is suspected but not confirmed. Forty years ago, there was ten times the number of Moose as there are now.

   Bear scat up the trail I walked after setting up camp, but no sign of any animals. In this grassy area, it is challenging to identify footprints. I didn't see any sign in the mud at the lakeside. Maybe I will see some wildlife here, then perhaps not. That isn't quite right as I saw two Great Blue Herons fly in and land in a large tree across the bay I think it is a Sugar Maple, but

even with the binoculars I couldn't tell for sure what Maple it is.
There is something abut the color and the spread of the
branches, but nothing I can quite put words to as why it looks
like a Sugar Maple. There is no doubt that they are Herons, that
is not under question. What magnificent birds, it feels like they
are telling me something.

Great Blue Heron

Often seen wading—
Marshlands and shallow water
Ponds, rivers, lakes, tidelands
Long-thin legs, slim necks
Sharp beaks

Walking on two legs
Impeccable balance
Ability to progress and evolve
Capability to explore deeply
Standing strong and stable alone

Hunting singly piercing eatables
Aptitude to explore deeply
Through water connected
While exploring the earth
Constantly vigilant

Open to variety—lifestyle
Food, terrain, vegetation
Appearing to be dabbling
Staring, watching everything,
Motionless, planning, thinking

Waiting for the exact moment
Creating opportunity
Successful at all endeavors
One moment at a time
Each moment important

Unstructured, unpredictable
Knowing inherently the path
Uniquely beautiful
Open to possibilities
As they appear

Distinctive S curved neck
Swift in flight
Maneuvering with determination
Wisdom in the decisions
Alluring to watch

Heronry's of hundreds high in trees
Squeaking and creaking
Enjoying their
High-density living
Scenic waterfront views

Enjoying this private grassy campsite, planned to be on
Lake Secret tonight, but it is just too beautiful here to leave. I am
sure there are Moose close by, but I do not see any. So, it is no
Moose sighting on Gossip.
Goodnight,

Edna
Gossip Lake

September 22

Equinox
Feeling the fall
Boy Scouts

Dear Sister Ursula,

I pack up early and eat only trail-mix for breakfast and paddle the ten miles to the portage. Busy portage as I arrive six men with their three canoes are preparing to launch. I wait out on the lake for them to leave. More people are arriving via the trail from Secret. It is a warm day while in the sun and quite crispy in the shade. The trail was through the trees, easy walk, but cold. Too warm in the sun, chilly even packing loads through the trees, it definitely feels like fall.

The group was Boy Scouts, a total of seven canoes. I quizzed the boys as they passed. It was fun. The leader who was sweeping up the rear put down his load as I entered the clearing at Secret and asked me, "Come back over to Gossip and join us for lunch, it should be ready in about half an hour. The boys are amazed you know so much about Boy Scouts, and I am embarrassed that they don't know the answers to some of your questions."

"I have a question, and you will know the answer. How is it your boys are out of school?"

"Easy, quick answer, the school has an emergency closure because of a septic problem. Matt is a teacher at the school, so he has the time. His three boys are part of the troop, and my two boys are also part of the troop. He is the scoutmaster, and I am the treasurer. I can get away because my wife will watch the business while I am gone. I can go as long as I take the boys with me. I think that was more information than you were looking for with your simple question. I have been known to talk too much."

"How many boys do you have total in the troop? You have twelve with you."

"Only two boys couldn't come, one has parents that will not let him do anything during football season that might limit his time on the field, and camping may bring on a cold or injury. Again too much information. They are great parents, looking for scholarships for college. The other boy has a broken arm in a cast. His dad wanted to come anyway, but that didn't fly well with the mom."

Through my laughs, I say, "That is too much information." Nothing would come out but laughter.

His reply was, "How about lunching with us?"

"I would love to lunch with all of you. I need to carry over another load of gear. I will be over in about twenty minutes."

It was fun, and the boys made individual beef stew in aluminum foil. Not burnt, cooked perfectly. They quizzed me about Boy Scout facts. Three of the boys would huddle and figure out a question that they thought was difficult and that they knew the answer to, and when I knew the answer, they would be shocked. "How did you know that?"

I didn't tell them that I had excellent hearing and could hear them deciding on the answer. Mostly I knew the answer, but it was fun giving the answer word for word that the boys figured the was correct answer. Then they brought out the Chocolate Bars. Everyone was given a huge bar, a real monster. They gave me one, and I asked if I eat it who doesn't get one. That brought out a huge roar and a gleeful explanation that they had enough

147

for everyone to have two every day and enough for s'mores as well.

"Thank you for the lunch and the great entertainment. Also, for the candy bar, I hope you have a wonderful autumn equinox and the first day of fall." I headed to Lake Secret with my last load of supplies and my candy bar.

The campground was a couple of hours off, and I still had plenty of daylight left. I thought about traveling with the boys on campouts, and they do keep it busy and entertaining. Sure is a different experience than going alone.

The Autumn Equinox deserves my attention, especially this year, while I am here to experience the daylight diminishing to darkness moment by moment. I am using my flashlights so much more it is diminishing my power supply. Less daylight to charge and more usage. Barly keeping up for the use of the computer for writing and limited lights.

Today is the day to decide about what to getting rid of by the release of unwanted beliefs and emotional baggage. There are plenty to choose from in the old habits. I will think about it today and write tonight on my decisions.

I am looking forward to hearing the secrets that the lake has to whisper to me. It seems perfect to be on Secret Lake today.

The list of gratefulness is long; mostly, I am so happy to be on this trip and healthy. I certainly have had many things to be grateful for on this trip topping out the abundance here in the boundary waters and for all I have. It was to be a day to reflect, and it certainly has been. In many ways, it has been the same as every day here on the water, but with ritual and mind-fullness, it has been different. The water has spoken in its calm, silent way.

After a hike around the woods where I gathered a bag of pine cones, a bit of moss, a few pretty rocks, odd little things, and five wing feathers. I came back to camp to set up the altar and lit a fire to begin. I have decided to not wait until after dark to start. The clouds hare rolled in, and it smells like rain on the way. I have the two tarps up so I will remain reasonably dry, but it isn't warm, and the rain will not bring in a warmth that the sun earlier provided. The altar has a variety of leaves as a blanket over the ground with pine needles around the edges like a border keeping the items in so none can escape the reason they are here. I use the flint and steel as a symbol of simplicity, honoring the gift of fire. The flame starts small burning greedily toward the globs of pitch I put among the twigs I had gathered for instant fuel. I openly ask for health, abundance, and joy for the coming year. In moments the gentle flicker of flame turns into snapping and popping as the heat hits the bubbles of resin bring light into this semi-darkness.

I put past hurts into the fire one at a time using pine cones to symbolize each person I have hurt, my children, my friends, my parents, releasing the emotion around them and me. The cones still have their shape, but sit in the coals, as skeletons without pain and life. They are dried, beautiful, and haunting— reminding me of The Day of the Dead, honoring the ancestors, and inviting them back to celebrate family. It is an honorable tradition cooking all the favorite family foods, putting out pictures of those who have passed from living on earth — skeletons and ghosts from the past. Dia de Muertos.

My ceremony was simple. Burned chips of wood to rid myself of the feeling of being less than I should be--of not being perfect. Of aches and pains. Turned into being more of a grateful session. I then did affirmations for what is coming: continue to plan nature trips, to recognize all I have to be thankful, be aware of the beauty around me. I appreciate my health. Inner peace is always part of what I wish. These last few years, the balance for the earth to overcome is big on the list.

Huge difficulties for the world as the ice melts out from under the polar bears.

The day wasn't as I had expected. The surprises added to the enjoyment as did a couple of bites off of the chocolate bar.

Goodnight,
Edna

Gossip to Secret Lake

September 23

Instant Autumn
National Park Lookout Trail, 2 miles.
Trees color

Dear Sister Ursula,

   I hear rustling of a small animal under me as I awake in my
hammock. It is not quite light. I sense the wind high in the trees.
I peek out the front—too dark to see clearly, but I can hear the
water. I slip out and walk the short distance to the beach. The
water is alive with whitecaps, the waves hitting the shore with
exuberance. I adjust from looking forward to packing the canoe
and getting out on the lake—to deciding to explore the hillside.
The map had shown a trail leading through the trees just around
the bend; I shall explore by land today. If I leave soon, I will be
able to watch the sunrise from the cliff.
   My vacation time is coming to an end; I am almost done
with my trip only a couple more days on my journey. I am not in
a rush to get back to civilization. I have to be reasonable in my
thinking, but I don't feel complete yet; I am considering staying
a little longer than planned. I still have food, I am fine, but fall is
coming the temperatures are lower a little every day, and I
especially feel it in the evenings. Part of the reason to spend time
at the Boundary Waters in this season is to see the tree colors in
all their splendor, but here it is nearing the end of my journey,
and the only color is a few deep red large-leaf maples scattered
across the forest. I am not disappointed in my trip, just a little in
not being here for the fall colors. I am pleased beyond my

151

expectation of how special these two months would be. The beauty I have witnessed at each bend and turn from lake to lake.

For the past week, I have been enjoying the few scattered Red Acer's. Glorious in their brilliance. The abundance of green surrounding them highlighted each individual tree. Exciting and splendid as they are, I am becoming resigned to the fact that I will not have the privilege of seeing the whole landscape in full color.

It will be an all-day hiking trip, no thought of leaving today—today will be off into the woods. The sunlight is beginning to show on the horizon; I will walk for a couple of hours before breakfast. I have been indecisive about what to pack for the day.

Two liters of water will be enough. It isn't hot, enough food for three meals and two snacks. Changing my mind on what to take, I settle on: the bug suit, rain gear, gloves, sunscreen, binoculars, food, and for good measure, I decided to add another liter of water. In my inefficiency, I have put up and taken down the stash out of the tree three times. Oh, well, not a big thing. Bringing to mind that I haven't been going on many hikes on this trip.

I must have enough since the backpack is full. If for any reason, I cannot make it back and need to spend the night I will be okay, well, with that thought, I stuff in my angora sweater—I will be plenty warm.

Pushing through the brush, making my way over to the Park trail was rough going, with so many downed trees and a tangle of low vegetation on the edge of the lake made for difficult walking. The hiking trail was easy to find, I walked right onto it, next to a sign that said, "National Park Lookout Trail, 2 miles." It appears to be a well-known lookout, a destination point.

Only by many people walking on this trail has it become a well-worn path. A touch of fear appears. I am now a bit worried about the possibility of undesirable encounters with people. I have not seen another canoe nor heard any human sounds. I think this is an irrational fear; I have only met fun and desirable people. Stop this thinking and get on with the enjoyment of the day.

The trail is not steep, but a continuous upward grade. I break out onto a huge boulder, at least sixty feet across, where it is evident via an old stain on the rock where people have built small fires and a few empty plastic water bottles that there have been people coming here. Off to the right is a squarish rock that looks like a park bench. No one has put it there as it is way too large, but a perfect seat to observe the valley below. Miles and miles off to the left lies the seemingly endless foliage of many shades of green. The Red Acer's stand out in their deep red, almost evenly spaced dotting the landscape. I am not sure what their real name is, but these are the ones we have always called Red Acer's, different from the Sugar Maples we tapped for maple syrup, and different from these Swamp Maples that cover the landscape. Off to the right is the lake between the Canadian and the US shore. The sunlight is amplifying the beauty reflecting off of the waves heading for the opposite shore.

It is a simple breakfast of cold pancakes, leftover from yesterday morning, dipped in a honey raspberry paste, a treat I have saved for a backpacking meal, and today is that day. I am relishing each bite as I look over the cliff and watch the sunrise.

Second National Park sign, "Upper Lookout 4.3 miles". I can see off across the valley what appears to be another boulder lookout, maybe that is it—maybe not. It seems further away than 4.3 miles. It appears that it will continue to be a gentle, slow, and steady incline. There are Foxgloves still in bloom in the shadow of the trees, just the last few purple bells on the top. Relaxed walking—the trail is dry, no steep rocks to climb, the trail bumps out to the edge of the valley, opening up to the fantastic view. It is glorious; everything about the whole view, the hillsides and valley have a hue, just a hint of yellow.

Back onto the trail, it has gotten a little steeper, not as well-worn. Branches and tall grass infringe on the path, but it is still a very recognizable trail. Only going over the huge boulders is it questionable where the trail exits into the foliage. Arriving at the Upper Lookout, I sit and eat my Trail mix of fruit and nuts. The trees are turning orange, not just a hint anymore, but the whole forest is a quarter orange. The wind has subsided, and the bugs have emerged. I put on my bug suit and sit and enjoy the view. I can almost see the maples turning orange. I know I can, well I could if I could focus on one leaf, I would see it change, but I lack the ability to make a comparison of what I saw a minute ago to what I see now. But it is different; all of the trees are doing this together, communicating and joining in a communal activity.

One scorching sunny July day, I was sitting on my porch swing, observing my vegetable garden. I had a small patch of corn just a couple of feet from the front steps. I sat there for two hours and watched the corn grow. It was different as it wasn't communications between plants. It was an individual plant stretching out and getting taller an inch at a time. In its way up it would do so in an explosion of energy; it was an over the top fascination experience. Today is on same level of observation—extraordinarily different but as educationally exciting.

I sat in my bug suit for an hour or so, the sun wasn't quite overhead when I arrived, and now it is beyond straight up; it has been at least an hour. I study the trees, and I estimate the percentage of orange. No real pattern to the areas that are more orange than others, but there are some places more and some places less than fifty percent. It isn't based on the sun, as not only those in the sun or in the shade are acting more together, but those on top of the hill and in the valleys shaded by their location all of them are of the same intentions a fast change in just a few hours it has gone from green to half orange.

It is time to continue my hike, Park sign reads. "Rim Circle 3.2 miles." Nothing shows on my little map, but it says circle, so it will, I hope, bring me back here. I have climbed in about six miles; I can turn back here or do the rim and then walk back. I have at least six more hours before dark—plenty of time to do the nine miles, the decision is—do I hike or sit and watch? I don't want to leave my newly acquired home, where I am observing the terrain changing before my eyes, but I also want to do the rim.

I decide to stay and watch; it continues to change, faster trail. I leave the pile of empty drinking bottles I picked up on the first stop in a pile near the entrance of the trail, as a marker for when I get back, so I know for sure I am in this spot to look for the trail down to my camp. As I head out, I think the view will open up in a quarter of a mile away, allotting a different view. It is remarkable I am now walking through an orange colored maple forest. Not so much underbrush up here. Spectacular; what a privilege to be observing this unique event. I will walk the rim.

The trail around the rim has open areas every few hundred feet, making for a continuously changing view of the hillside turning orange. When I reach the first lookout and sit on the bench overlooking the valley, there is no green left on the maple trees. Only a little green from the Pine Trees stand out by dotting the landscape. I sit and watch the sun lowering in the sky and eat my dinner of canned sockeye salmon and crisp-bread with just a sprinkle of spices. There are a few dates planned for dessert, but I feel so full of orange color that I am not interested in eating more—maybe after I walk back to camp.

Sister Ursula today has proven to be dramatically spectacular. My information bank on my computer says that science has proven that some plants communicate through their roots. I wonder if that is the only way they communicate. I certainly can see that they communicate. How isn't as obvious.

Goodnight,
Edna

Maple Trees Turning

Secret Lake

September 24

Beaver Bay
Last packet of strawberry jam
Last day on the water.

Dear Sister Ursula,

I am in the same camp as yesterday morning, and I awaken to the same rustling of small animals as I did yesterday. Today I continue to lie in the hammock and think about the fact that today is my last day of my paddle and portage canoe trip on the Boundary Waters. Today I will portage to Snowbank Lake. I will look for the Beaver house before I get to the portage. I was told by the twins that there might be a dam there as well. They didn't see it, but they were told that there was a beaver dam.

I will eat my last packet of strawberry jam with pancakes this morning. I have eaten the contents of every can. I have a duffel full of recycling, which clanks and jingles when I move it in and out of the canoe. I also have a gallon Ziplock half full of non-recyclable items, of which half of it is bottle caps I have picked up along the way.

As I paddled along the shore, a canoe with two men came closer to me so they could tell me about a beaver lodge off to the left just after the campsite up a small stream. They saw several Beavers dragging branches through the water. I will look for the Beaver house before I get to the portage. They were not sure, but there may be a dam there as well—this became my destination.

The twins had mentioned that there is a beaver lodge off to the left just after the campsite up a small stream. They saw several beavers dragging branches through the water — my destination point.

I pull up to what I believe to be Beaver Bay. It looks the same as the rest of the lake, tall grassy encroaching out into the lake. I paddle straight in towards the shore—no beaver dam or house to be seen. Drift up the lake and continue around the next point. I come upon two canoes pointing towards a beaver who is swimming with a branch across the open water towards them. He must be used to people in canoes watching him as he seems undisturbed. I come up alongside a canoe, and the man in the back reaches out to offer me the end of his paddle to raft up to his canoe. I surprise myself and raft up to watch the show.

"We have been here for about two hours watching; there are four beavers dragging in branches. We heard the crash of a tree hitting the water as we came around the point." He points to a nearby point of land a short distance off. Towards the direction I am heading. "We launched the beginning of our trip this morning. We had no idea it would be so entertaining in the first hours of our trip."

"I have only seen one other beaver house on my trip, and he went down and didn't come back up," I reply.

"My boys are so engrossed that they don't want to leave watching the building of the food supply for the winter. The younger boy, the one with the red cap, did a paper on Beavers last year in his science class. Spent months researching, it is his third year at college and would like to make beavers his life work. I have no idea how to go about doing that, but I know nothing about work opportunities in science. I am an insurance salesman with no education; I just took a job to earn a living. I am a good salesperson, and I like talking to people."

I don't say anything, I just smile and nod.

"You guessed that, didn't you?"

The woman in the front of the canoe turns towards me and says, "Hello, the Beavers don't seem to mind us talking. They are busy with their lives. I am expecting something to spook them, and with a loud slap of a tail, they will all disappear. College starts for the boys next week, and we will be back to our winter routine being busy as Beavers, and we will have this day to look back on as the best thing we could be doing with our lives. Watching the Beavers in this gorgeous setting, sitting in our canoes with the warmth of the sun on our shoulders."

I too am not in any hurry to move on to something else. Watching the Beavers is a graceful motion.

One of the Beavers stops swimming and raises himself to look directly at the boys. A moment of stillness, as if time itself stopped and then the tail hits the water, and the magic of watching the Beavers is over.

"Dad, I got the best photos imaginable of the Beavers with my GoPro. This is the best, thanks for making this trip happen. I know I gave you a hard time as I thought I would be better off spending my time doing my textbook reading than paddling and relaxing," the red cap boy said as they came up alongside their parent's canoe.

I backed off and headed west. My lunch location also had people. A group of woman was reorganizing their canoes and having lunch when I stopped and took out my pancake with strawberry jam and trail mix for lunch.

As I sat looking out on the water finishing my lunch, one of the women came over to me to tell me about their group. Interesting that this was her reason to come and sit by me.

"This is our first annual Women's Family Reunion at the Boundary Waters. At least that is my dream. I organized it and invited all the women of the family to join in on this adventure. We are not going to paddle very much each day. Our trip is for fourteen days. We started at Echo Trail went up along Moose River North, over towards Little Indian Sioux and then on to Crane. Planning on ending at the Arrowhead trail. Depending on how it all goes, we are thinking about going up the Granite River to Gunflint. It is said to be the prettiest portion of all of the boundary waters."

"How many women are in your family to invite?"

"I sent out thirty-five letters and received thirty answers saying it was a great idea. We have twenty female family members with us. Eight canoes and four riders. The young ones are most welcome as they will be the heart of keeping this going."

"Good luck to you getting this tradition going, you certainly have a great response for the first outing."

The portage onto Snowbank was crowded. I am trying to avoid people, but it is impossible as this is one of the primary entries and exits onto the Boundary Waters.

The portage was well worn, short, and an easy trail. In an hour, I was paddling towards the lodge that I will stay at tonight.

The cabin is cute with its' canoeing motif, is clean and has a soaker tub and a refrigerator with complimentary treats, a variety of pop, a cheese plate, and a bowl of nuts and dried fruit. I don't drink pop, I don't eat dairy. But the nuts and dried fruit were different than the trail mix I had eaten daily, so I devoured all of it. I am very much missing being outside—feels stuffy and as if the air has no oxygen in it.

Dropping off the canoe was simple, and my reservations were indeed available. I was able to make arrangements for a ride early in the morning to catch my ride into Ely transit stop at the Senior Center. The bus leaves at eight a.m. to Virginia. I don't know how I am going to get to Minneapolis from Virginia.

Maybe rent a car, take an Uber to Duluth, or hitchhike. There is a bus from Duluth once I get there.

I have many mixed feelings about the trip being over. I will sleep on it: a very comfortable bed and soft, cozy down comforter.

Goodnight,
Edna

Silent to Snowbank Lake

September 25

Getting on the Bus
Leaving Ely

Dear Sister Ursula,

Climbing onto the bus for the ride from Ely to the airport puts a finality to the trip. The driver looked at my pile of gear and said, "Are you, Edna?"

"I sure am."

"Your storage space is right behind me."

"Thanks, I get on and put two bags behind the seat and get off the bus for the next load. Two other riders get on and pay their fare. I deposit two more bags behind the driver. I am pleased it will all fit. A young man appears with my two small packs from my pile. I thank him and retrieve the last duffel. I had reserved storage space when I called and paid a five-dollar deposit—which is a strange thing. I wasn't able to purchase a ticket for myself, but when I arrived, the driver credited my fare the five dollars. Made sense to them, and there was room for my baggage, the driver kept it for me because I had prepaid for space.

I look around at the few empty seats on this nearly full local transit. A teen boy with earbuds is sprawled over both seats. A woman with two children in the seat in front of her has a disarray of stuff spilling onto the aisle. A middle-aged man is reading a newspaper. An elderly woman is dressed to the nines. She is probably younger than me, but I don't see her as a desirable seat companion. I continued my search for a seat. I spot a Danner hiking boot in the aisle below an Eddie Bauer pant leg. As I walked closer, the shirt wasn't a surprise, a Woolrich Scotch plaid flannel button-down over a turtleneck. Perfect—his appearance is of an outdoorsman who just spent a few weeks in the backcountry.

Not a word was said; he just stood up and let me into the window seat.

"You don't look as scruffy as I do, but my guess is you just got off of the water. How long have you been paddling?"

The conversation was desirable and comfortable, so much to share with someone that just got off the water. "Didn't see a Moose all the while I was out. How about you?"

Goodnight,
Edna

About The Author

Perrilee Pizzini

You may also enjoy her first book "Alone on the Taiga" about time she spent in a cabin in the U.S. Wrangell Saint Elias National Park.

She has since an early age enjoyed the beauty and wonders of the earth. The rugged mountain outlines against the clouded sky, the trees bending in the wind. Insects swarming, fish jumping leaving droplets spraying across the smooth lake. Life has endless intrigues to investigate and ponder: fascinating, mysterious, and gripping.

Made in the USA
Las Vegas, NV
04 October 2022